Sleuths & Seductions

by

Andrea Knight

Copyright © 2023

All rights reserved. No part of this publication may be reproduced, distributed, or transmitted in any form or by any means, including photocopying, recording, or other electronic or mechanical methods, without the prior written permission of the author.

Chapter 1

Diving headfirst into the seething soup of humanity that was London in 1882 was like trying to navigate an overpopulated anthill. Street vendors screamed like banshees about their subpar apples, horses were clopping around like they were fucking tap dancers, and the noisy confusion of chatter was enough to drive a saint to sin.

And right smack in the middle of this absolute circus, I was about to play ringmaster.

My eyes, sharp as a hawk, fell on this spindly old dame, hunched over like she'd misplaced her spine. In her grip was a purse, clutched tighter than a virgin's virtue, though I feared even her tightest grip was about as effective as a toddler's. She was so engrossed in her death march through the swarm of bodies, she didn't even notice the predator sneaking up on her. I clocked him immediately - the greedy glint in his eyes, the casual swagger that was a bit too casual. This wasn't your garden variety pickpocket; this was a seasoned purse pilferer, and granny was the lamb to his damned wolf.

Before you could say 'Petticoat Lane', the scruffy fucker made his move. A bump, a grab, and then he was off, galloping away like he'd just won the bloody lottery. He knew the streets like a rat knows the sewers, ducking and weaving through the throng like a Prosecco-fuelled partygoer.

Meanwhile, I was across the street, pawing over an antique book like some kind of literary pervert. But the second I spotted the theft, the book dropped from my hands and I was off like a bat out of hell. This cockwomble thought he could just snatch and dash? Not on my watch.

There I was, a well-turned-out lady in spectacular leather boots, hot-footing it after a man down the streets of London.

I could practically hear the whispers: "Who's the crazy bitch?" But I didn't give a rat's arse. My old spy reflexes were back in full swing, and the thrill of the chase was more intoxicating than a bottle of absinthe.

The bloke had the gall to look surprised when he saw me hot on his tail. Bet he wasn't expecting Elizabeth Templeton - mild-mannered bookstore owner by day, no-nonsense ass-kicker by night - to come after him. But I had a bag of tricks that would make a magician green with envy, and I was about to give this wanker a lesson he wouldn't forget.

I dodged, I weaved, I leapt over obstacles like the lovechild of a gazelle and a trapeze enthusiast. The bastard was fast, I had to admit, but he was as sloppy as a drunken butcher.

He tried to use the crowd as cover, but I was on his tail like a bad rash, leaping over a heap of burlap sacks like a hurdler. I could tell he was tiring, but I was just hitting my stride. After years of outrunning Russian mobsters and outmaneuvering Tunisian knife-wielders, this asshole was a walk in the park.

He scrambled into an alleyway, thinking the shadows could hide him, but I followed close behind. No escape now, you piece of shit. He spun around, pulling a rusty blade from his pocket, which I easily knocked away with a roundhouse kick that would make a ninja weep with joy. Then I slammed my elbow into his nose and he crumpled like a ragdoll, out cold. Textbook Templeton.

I stood over the groaning thief, chest heaving, filled with that post-fight rush. Quick as a viper, I snatched the purse from his limp hands. The elderly woman probably needed this back more than this scumbag needed the penny or two it contained. I left the fool where he lay - the coppers would find him eventually. Right now, I had a purse to return.

I approached the distraught woman who was tearfully recounting the crime to a bobby. As soon as she saw me holding out her purse, relief washed over her face.

"Here you are, ma'am. Some rotten luck back there but I believe this belongs to you," I said with a smile.

She grasped the purse like it was her baby. "Oh bless you dear! However did you get it back?"

"I simply asked the lad and he was kind enough to return it," I replied. No need to mention my foot planted on his jugular at the time. "Do be careful around these parts."

"Of course, of course!" she said. "Thank you again, miss. Not many would go through such efforts for an old woman's purse."

"My pleasure," I said with a nod. And it was. Moments like this, using my skills for good, made this life worthwhile.

I left the woman with her gratitude and the bobby with a new imminent arrest and continued on my way. It was time to get back to my real job.

The sign reading "Templeton's Tales" came into view and I stepped through the doors of the quaint bookshop I called my own.

The scent of aged paper and leather bindings welcomed me as it always did. I took a deep breath, feeling some of the tension dissipate from my shoulders. Here in this space, filled with literary treasures and memories, I was home.

I made my way through the shop, fingers trailing over the spines of beloved books. There was no chaos here, no crimes to stop or villains to pursue. Just endless stories waiting to be discovered.

In the back corner sat my sanctuary, a cozy office furnished with artifacts from my previous life—maps of exotic cities I'd traveled, disguises and gadgets from my spy days, fading photographs of people I'd loved and lost—it was part museum, part mausoleum; a place to remember the crazy risks I'd taken, the narrow escapes, the adventures and heartbreaks. I missed the thrill like hell. But I'd earned this quieter life, and the solitude that came with it.

The soft tinkling of the bell above the shop door startled me from my thoughts. I stepped out of my office to see who had entered. A smile involuntarily twitched at the corners of my lips at the sight of the familiar figure sauntering between the shelves like he owned the place.

Thomas Callahan, one of my most regular customers. Not to mention as intriguing as a locked diary in a teenage girl's bedroom.

As he perused the shelves, I allowed myself a moment to admire the view.

Thomas cut a striking figure. As he brushed his fingers over the book spines with the gentle reverence of a priest at communion, I seized my chance to ogle. And ogle I did. The man was a sight to behold. Over six feet tall, he had a rugged attractiveness, with features carved like a Greek god's, and his hair, a salt-and-pepper mess, looked like it had been styled by a windstorm. But it was those eyes, crystal blue and hinting at a thousand unsolved puzzles, that had me wanting to play detective.

When he glanced up and caught me watching him, his mouth lifted in a crooked grin.

"See something you like, Miss Templeton?" His deep voice held a note of amusement.

I cocked an eyebrow at him. "Perhaps. Though I can hardly admire the merchandise with a customer obstructing my view."

He laughed, rich and warm. The sound sent a pleasant tingle down my spine. Our flirtatious banter had become a comfortable rhythm whenever he visited the shop. And visit he did, sometimes two or three times a week, always with a smile and a teasing remark that left me off-balance.

Thomas moved away from the shelves he'd been browsing and leaned one hip against the counter where I stood.

"And how are you this fine day, Miss Templeton?"

"Oh, can't complain," I replied breezily, stacking my catalog cards into a neat pile. "Business is booming, the sun is shining, and I've got a half-priced first edition awaiting inspection in the bargain bin. What more could a girl want?"

"Hmm, I might have a few suggestions."

His voice had dropped even more, velvety smooth. The

teasing glimmer in his eyes sent a spike of heat through my core. I shifted, suddenly feeling flushed. Damn the man for having such an effect on me.

I studiously avoided meeting his gaze, pretending great interest in aligning my pencil just so atop a stack of papers.

"Do you now? Pray tell, what does a man of your…particular interests suggest I need?"

Out of the corner of my eye, I saw him lean closer, forearms braced on the counter. His sleeve brushed mine, and I had to suppress a shiver at the contact.

"Well," he nearly purred, "for starters, I think you could use a bit more excitement in your life."

My eyes snapped to his. I bristled. "Are you implying my life lacks excitement, Mr. Callahan?"

He held up a placating hand. "Not at all. I merely meant that even the most contented creature needs a bit of…adventure now and then." One dark eyebrow arched meaningfully. "Variety is the spice of life, or so they say."

I knew he was baiting me, trying to get a rise. But I refused to let him fluster me.

"I have all the excitement I need here, thank you. The print world is adventure enough for me."

"Is that so?" He leaned in, voice dropping conspiratorially. "I don't believe you. I think there's more to you than meets the eye, Miss Elizabeth Templeton."

My breath caught at his use of my first name. It sounded sinfully intimate on his lips. For one wild moment an image rose in my mind – Thomas murmuring my name, his body pressing mine into the mattress…

Arousal bloomed hot and urgent between my legs. I scrambled for composure.

"You seem determined to invent hidden facets of my character, Mr. Callahan," I said, with a sly smile. "I'm afraid the real me is quite dull by comparison."

His eyes searched my face for a long moment. "No," he replied finally. "You're anything but dull."

Before I could respond, he straightened abruptly. "Well, I suppose I should stop pestering you. Wouldn't want to keep you from your work."

The flirtatious mood evaporated. I bit my lip, already missing our verbal sparring. But refusing to beg for his company, I simply nodded.

"Let me know if you need any assistance finding something."

"Will do." With a wink and a grin, he sauntered back into the stacks, whistling softly.

I released a breath. The man was positively maddening. And enticing. And confusing as hell. One moment he was flirting shamelessly, his voice a seductive caress. The next he was friendly but distant, giving no indication he wanted more from me than casual banter.

I yearned to unravel the mystery that was Thomas Callahan. What lay beneath that charming exterior? Was he genuinely interested, or was I just a passing amusement?

Sighing, I turned my focus back to my work. Better not to waste time daydreaming. Nothing would come of it anyway. I'd vowed long ago not to let anyone get too close. It was better—safer—to devote myself to my haven here. Alone.

The minutes passed in amiable silence, broken only by the shuffle of pages and occasional creak of old floorboards under Thomas's feet. I soon lost myself in updating the catalog, determinedly keeping my eyes averted whenever I heard Thomas move to a new section.

After nearly an hour, he appeared at the counter once more, several books tucked under one arm.

"Find what you were looking for?" I asked, avoiding his gaze.

"Oh yes. Although…"

He trailed off. When I reluctantly met his eyes, I was startled by the intensity in them. My breath caught.

"Although?"

"Although I'm still searching for something far more elusive." He paused, then added softly, "Something infinitely more valuable."

I stared at him, heart pounding. Surely he didn't mean....

I broke our gaze and reached mechanically for the books he'd set on the counter. As I recorded them in the ledger, I struggled to rein in my seesawing emotions.

"Shakespeare," I said. "I took you for more of a Keats man."

Thomas chuckled, his eyes glinting. "What can I say, I'm full of surprises. One sonnet in particular struck my fancy."

He flipped open the book, reciting with feeling:

"Shall I compare thee to a summer's day?

Thou art more lovely and more temperate..."

Heat rose in me as his gaze lingered. Thomas absolutely delighted in flustering me.

"Are you reciting Shakespeare to woo me, Mr. Callahan?" I asked pointedly, arching an eyebrow.

"That depends, is it working?"

He leaned in over the counter. I met his eyes defiantly, refusing to be swayed by his charms.

"It will take more than pretty words to win my favor," I said.

Thomas laughed, straightening back up. "I enjoy a challenge. Perhaps you'll join me for dinner tonight and I can properly convince you?"

The thought of a romantic dinner under the bloody stars with this devilishly attractive scoundrel was almost more than I could take. But it was a risky move where I could potentially spill my sordid past over a fancy glass of wine. I had secrets that could make a priest blush and a sailor blush harder. And I wasn't about to spill my guts to some charming Casanova who could use it against me.

But damn, he was a sight for sore eyes. With his chiseled jawline that could cut diamonds and a smile that could melt the skirt off a lady saint, he had me weak in the knees. I could practically feel his magnetic charm pulling me in, making me forget all about my internal warning bells.

It was a hard pill to swallow, like a bitter goddamn horse tranquilizer, really, but sometimes self-preservation had to take priority over fleeting pleasures.

But let me tell you, it took all the strength I had to resist the allure of his smoldering gaze and that mischievous twinkle in his eye. I had to remind myself that I was a force to be reckoned with, a badass who had survived more shit than a sewer rat.

"Another night perhaps," I demurred. "I have plans this evening that I cannot break."

It wasn't exactly a lie, though my only real plan was to avoid complications.

Thomas sighed in exaggerated disappointment. "You wound me. But I am nothing if not persistent," he said, paying for his books. "I'll win you over yet, even if takes reciting every sonnet I know."

"I look forward to seeing you try," I replied, unable to hide my grin.

With a parting tip of his hat, Thomas turned and left, the shop bell tinkling behind him. I watched him go, his confident stride and broad shoulders cutting a hell of a silhouette.

Once alone, I let out a slow breath, fanning myself from the lingering heat of our exchange. As much as I fought to deny it, something about Thomas Callahan left me flushed and breathless in ways I hadn't felt in years. A complicated, dangerous reaction given my history.

Shaking off the encounter, I retreated to my office in the back of the shop. It was my sanctuary, filled with artifacts from my past adventures. How different from the guarded, solitary book shop owner I was now. I'd given up that world of underground intrigue for a quiet, unassuming life.

It was safer this way.

Settling into my leather armchair, I tried focusing on the stack of new acquisitions I needed to catalog. But my mind kept drifting back to Thomas. I imagined his rugged features in the glow of candlelight, a bottle of wine shared between us. His lips meeting mine, his hands tangled in my hair...

A blush rose on my cheeks. I was acting like a bloody smitten schoolgirl, distracted by daydreams. I shook my head, attempting to clear away the lingering images. Thomas was an intriguing man, but I knew firsthand how treacherous desire could be. My past was littered with broken hearts, betrayal, and lives destroyed. Anonymity was my armor, this bookshop my sanctuary.

A sudden crash jarred me, my heart jolting into an instantaneous jig. I leapt to my feet, senses razor sharp. The noise had come from the front of the shop. Moving to the curtained doorway with all the grace of a drunken swan in heels, I peered out onto the sales floor onto what can only be described as a crime scene—if the crime was murdering innocent decor.

There stood the apparent vase-assassin - a young woman with chestnut hair that looked like it had been styled by a tornado and cheeks streaked with enough tears to water a half-dead geranium. The remains of what used to be a vase were scattered around her.

Her eyes, big and round, lifted and met mine. Fright flickered in them like she'd seen a ghost, or was afraid she was about to become on. Great. Not only did I have to deal with the shattered remains of, let's face it, an ugly ass vase, but also play counselor to the weeping willow in torn stockings.

"Please...you have to help me," she said, her voice trembling.

I stepped forward, surveying her with a practiced eye. She was clearly distraught, her clothing torn and a livid bruise forming on her wrist. Dark secrets seemed to swirl in her eyes, a story that went beyond this terrified facade. I knew the look all too well.

My heart went out to her, even as my instincts screamed to protect the peace I'd worked so hard to build. But I couldn't turn away a woman so obviously in need.

"It's alright, you're safe here," I said gently. "Tell me what happened."

The young woman sucked in a shuddering breath. "My name is Amelia. I...I'm being followed, hunted by a dangerous man." Her eyes darted about like a cornered animal's. "I didn't know where else to turn."

I hesitated, warring with myself. Getting involved would only lead to trouble. And yet, seeing her fear, I felt a pang of responsibility.

"Come, let's get you settled with some tea," I said, making up my mind. I would try to help her...discretely.

As I ushered her into my private office, my mind raced. Whoever this girl had tangled with, they meant business. And I knew better than most how to handle men who hid in shadows. Maybe if I was careful, I could aid her without revealing too many of my own secrets. Some battles still must be fought, after all.

As Amelia began recounting her story, I steeled myself. Danger was afoot, and with it, the kinds of complications I dreaded most.

Chapter 2

"I was told...that is, I heard..." Amelia trailed off, eyes darting around as if afraid we were being watched.

I softened my voice further. "It's alright. Whatever you need to say, this is a safe place."

Amelia took a shaky breath, eyes glistening. "I was told you might be able to help me."

Fuck.

I quickly assessed the situation. Young, clearly been beaten, clothes torn and dirtied, seeking help but scared to ask it - she was likely a victim of the seedy underbelly of this city that I knew far too well. The question was, what did she think I could do about it?

"Tell me what happened, Amelia," I said softly once she'd taken a few sips of tea.

Her slim shoulders trembled. "It started a fortnight ago," she whispered. "Odd things, small at first. A man watching me as I shopped at the bakery in the morning. Footsteps echoing mine at night on my way home from the dress shop where I work. A feeling of being watched, even in my own home."

My jaw tightened, but I kept silent, letting her continue her story.

"At first I thought I was imagining things. But then..." Her voice dropped, and she clutched her sleeve where I could see bruises peeking out. "Two nights ago, on my way home, a man grabbed me and pulled me into an alley."

"Did you get a look at him?" I asked.

She shook her head, eyes brimming with tears. "It was dark, and he wore a cloak. But he..." She choked back a sob, face crumpling. "He said I belonged to Lord Stanton now. That I'd better do as he commanded or he'd..."

The name hit me like a blow. Lord Marcus Stanton. A goddamn hurricane of ruthlessness, reigning over both high society and the grimy underbelly of this city. His reputation for cruelty was well-earned. If he had targeted this poor young woman...

And what kind of sick bastard goes after a defenseless young woman, anyway? I clenched my fists, ready to rain a shitstorm of vengeance on the sadistic bastard. I wanted to make Lord Stanton learn that messing with me was like sticking his dick in a hornet's nest. But before I could unleash my wrath upon the aristocratic prick, I needed to know what the fuck he was up to with this poor woman, and I needed to know it yesterday.

Amelia was sobbing quietly now, face buried in her hands. I poured more tea with a steadiness I did not feel. The name rattled around inside my head. After so many years, it seemed the tendrils of my past were creeping back in. Try as I might to live a quiet, orderly life, evil could never be fully escaped

I steeled myself. This wasn't the moment for reminiscing or fear. This young woman needed my help. I gently grasped her hands in mine.

"Amelia, listen to me. You're safe here. I won't let Lord Stanton or his men harm you any further, I promise you that." She looked up, a spark of hope flickering in her red-rimmed eyes.

"But how?" she whispered hoarsely.

I gave her a wry half-smile. "Let's just say I'm not unacquainted with men like him." I stood briskly and went to bolt the shop door and flip the sign to 'Closed.' When I returned, Amelia was watching me with a hint of wariness.

"So, the rumors are true then? They say you're more than just a bookshop owner. That you've helped people, women like me, who had nowhere left to turn."

Damn gossips. Couldn't leave well enough alone.

I kept my face carefully composed. "As I said, you're safe here. No need to worry about rumors."

The truth was, I didn't help people anymore. Hadn't for a long time. I'd left that life behind. I was just a bookshop owner, living a safe, quiet life.

That's what I told myself, anyway.

But somehow my reputation had found me.

Though looking into this frightened young woman's eyes, I felt the long-slumbering spark of anger deep inside flicker to life again. Anger at men like Lord Stanton who used their power to take what they wanted and destroyed lives without a second thought.

Could I really stand by and do nothing?

I took a slow breath, then met Amelia's gaze directly. "Tell me everything you know about Lord Stanton. His habits, his associates, anyplace you've seen his men frequent. I will look into this matter, but you must promise me you'll speak of this to no one. Understood?"

Amelia let out a choked breath, eyes shining with gratitude now. "Oh thank you, Miss Templeton! Thank you, bless you for helping me." She clutched my hands again. "I knew those rumors must be true. They say you've brought terrible men to justice before, men everyone else was too afraid to stand up to. They say..."

I held up a hand. "That's quite enough. The past is the past. What matters now is making sure Lord Stanton doesn't lay a hand on you again."

We spent the next hour going over everything Amelia knew about Stanton and his operations. She didn't have much, but every detail could prove useful.

I pressed some coins into her palm and instructed her to take a carriage to an inn I knew on the outskirts of the city. "Stay out of sight and trust no one until you hear from me again," I told her.

She nodded, eyes brimming with tears. Impulsively, I pulled her into a quick embrace.

"Be strong, Amelia. I will do everything in my power to resolve this situation. Do not give up hope."

She gave me a tremulous smile and slipped out the door.

The next morning, sun filtered in through the windows of my bookshop like it thought it was God's gift to the color palette. Mornings like these were my favorite -feeling the slow burn of tea down my throat and simply thinking, basking in the kind of quiet where you can actually hear your own deliciously debauched thoughts.

But peace was as rare as a nun in a brothel, and the door slammed open like it had been kicked in by a battering ram. In snuck my little spymaster-in-training, right on the devil's heels.

"Morning, Miss Elizabeth!" Jacob exploded into the room, tossing his sandy hair like he was the star of some shampoo ad. The kid was like a damn puppy on twelve cups of coffee, and I couldn't help but love him. He had that kind of eager face that says, "I'll fetch your slippers or your secrets, just say the word."

But he wasn't just another adorable face; the lad was sharp as a tack.

"Got any work for me today?"

Despite myself, I felt the corners of my mouth turn up. Jacob's cheer was infectious. He was a good kid - smart, observant, with a knack for being in the right place at the right time to overhear a useful whisper or two. Plus, he knew how to keep his mouth shut, which was even more important in my line of work.

"I think I've got just the job for you," I said, reaching below the counter to grab a carefully wrapped package. Discrete deliveries were Jacob's specialty. The kid could maneuver through the London streets like a fish through water - slipping unseen through crowds, darting down back alleys, dropping a parcel where it needed to go without a soul being any the wiser.

I flashed him a sly smile. "Just a little something," I say, and slid him a package, all wrapped up like a virgin on her wedding night.

Jacob's eyes lit up, his fingers twitching eagerly. "Hot tip?" he asked.

I shrugged, keeping my face neutral. "Could be something, could be nothing. Take it to Anastasia, and don't let anyone see you."

He stuffed it in his coat like he was hiding dirty little secrets. But then, the little blighter stalled, like he had an itch he couldn't scratch.

"Oh, right, almost slipped my mind," he said, suddenly all grave, like he was about to tell me the pub's run out of gin. "Down by the docks—some chaps gabbing about girls vanishing. Poor things, here today, gone tomorrow. No bloody clue why."

The chill that ran down my spine wasn't from the morning air.

"Probably just drunken tales, Jacob," I said lightly. "You know how people love to spin wild stories after a few pints. I wouldn't fret about it too much."

Jacob nodded again, though he still seemed uneasy. "You're probably right. Well, anyway, I best be off. See you this afternoon, Miss Elizabeth!"

With that, he darted out the door and down the street, package tucked close beneath his coat. I watched him disappear around a corner before I let the neutral mask slip from my face.

Bloody hell. This was not good.

I stood and started shelving books to keep my hands busy, hoping the mind-numbing task would quiet my racing thoughts. I should have known my simple life here was too good to last. It seemed my past was catching up to me once again no matter how hard I tried to outrun it.

How many bloody years had it been since I'd traded in danger, intrigue, and heartbreak for the quiet thrill of a good book and a decent cuppa? Five?

The memories of that time still flashed through my mind in brilliant, chaotic fragments. I'd promised myself a clean break from the double-crosses, the bloodshed, the godforsaken secrecy. But here I was, still unable to fully break away. This bookshop and its quaint diversions were supposed to have been my clean escape.

I sighed. Maybe deep down I'd always known I could never really turn my back on the thrill and the mystery.

My gaze landed on a portrait hanging on the back wall, a relic from my reckless youth. That Elizabeth, wild and fierce, her eyes flashing with a spark that could ignite a bloody forest. The muted blue dress she wore looked so at odds with the coiled energy in her frame, like a wolf awkwardly stuffed into a sheep's wool. Looking into her eyes was like peering into the soul of a wildcat yearning for the untamed wilderness.

"Just stay calm," I muttered to myself. "You've outgrown that shit."

But even as I tried to convince myself, it felt about as genuine as a three quid note. Something about this situation with Amelia had cracked open that restless part inside me, sending all my suppressed memories and instincts roaring back to the surface. As much as I wanted to pretend otherwise, I knew I couldn't just brush this off and trust that others would handle it. That wasn't who I was. Or at least, who I used to be.

Right. That was enough wallowing for one day. I straightened up, squaring my shoulders. I may not be an active spy anymore, but I still had connections in this city - informants, society gossipers, and a handful of disgruntled housemaids with more dirt than a pigsty. It was time to see what information I could gather. If girls were truly disappearing and men like Lord Stanton were involved, I needed to find proof before I could act.

A glance at the clock told me my assistant, Oliver, should be rolling in soon to take over shop duty. Perfect. I needed to get out and shake off the cobwebs, even if it meant slipping back into my old skin. I pulled my hair into a bun as tight as a miser's purse strings, donned a cloak as dark as my past, and headed for the door.

Look out London - Elizabeth was back.

The scent of ale and unwashed bodies hit me like a sucker punch as I stepped into The Black Boar tavern, crinkling my nose in disgust. I paused just inside the doorway, letting my eyes adjust to the dim lighting as I scanned the crowded room. Rough wooden tables that looked like they hadn't been wiped since the Black Plague filled the space, packed cheek to jowl with laborers, sailors, and various unsavory characters. The cacophony of voices drowned out the crackling fire in the mammoth stone hearth, like a bunch of drunken hyenas trying to out-bellow each other.

I scanned the room, my eyes darting from one shady figure to another, trying to find my target.

Like a beacon of hope in the cesspool of debauchery, I spotted an empty stool at the end of the bar and made my way over, threading through the throng, dodging groping hands and spilled drinks. The bartender, a burly motherfucker with a beard that could rival a grizzly bear, gave me a skeptical once-over.

"Ain't often we get high-class ladies in here," he rumbled. "What'll it be, miss?"

I leaned in, lowering my voice to a sultry whisper that could make angels blush, and said, "Give me your strongest poison. I've had a day that would make a priest reach for a bottle of tequila." I slapped a few coins on the bar top.

The bartender grunted, his skepticism morphing into something resembling respect. He poured me a shot that looked like it could strip paint off a train car, and with a nod, he slid it across the bar. Raising it to my lips with a silent toast to the twisted fate that brought me to this wretched hive of scum and villainy, I knocked it back, relishing the burn.

The bartender refilled it without asking. I sipped the second one slowly, training my eyes on the door. If anyone knew the more sinister secrets behind the disappearances, they'd be here.

My eyes scanned the joint, searching for clues amidst the sea of degenerates. That's when I spotted them – a trio of rough-looking bastards huddled around a table near the roaring hearth. Their clothes were threadbare, speaking of hard labor and sweat-soaked toil, but their hands were smoother than a baby's ass. Too smooth for honest work.

I watched them trade furtive glances with a table of finely dressed gentlemen across the room, almost unnoticeable if you weren't looking for it. But my well-honed senses caught the subtle interplay instantly.

I rolled my shoulders, feeling the tension melt away like a hooker's morals on payday. This was my element – the thrill of the hunt, the chase for truth in this cesspool of deception.

An hour passed uneventfully until a lanky youth slid onto the stool next to mine, his movements fluid and graceful like a cat. My hand drifted to the dagger hidden in the folds of my cloak as I gave him a measured look. He met my gaze with a roguish smirk.

"Easy darling, I'm not looking for trouble." His voice was smooth, with an educated clip that seemed out of place. Up close, his fine clothes were tailored but worn, and I detected a hint of desperation lurking beneath his bravado. An aristocratic runaway perhaps, looking to numb his woes.

I relaxed my grip on the dagger. "Then you're in the wrong place, boy."

He flashed an easy grin. "Aren't we all?"

Before I could respond, the bartender thumped another glass down. "On the house," he muttered before lumbering away.

The youth picked up the glass, swirling the liquor beneath his nose. "An interesting choice for a lady."

I arched a brow. "And you have such expansive experience with ladies to make that assessment?"

"More than you might think." He took a sip, wincing slightly at the harsh taste.

"I'm no lady," I replied bluntly, tiring of verbal volleys. "You clearly want something. Out with it."

The direct approach had him averting his eyes. When he met my gaze again, the desperation was unveiled. "I'm...looking for work. Unconventional work for unconventional people. I heard this was the place to make such connections."

I studied him more closely, noting the wiry strength of his frame, the quick intelligence in his eyes. Most importantly, I noted the imposing signet ring on his left hand, bearing the crest of a noble family. He slid the hand out of view but the observation was made.

"Be careful playing games you don't understand," I said gently. "Before you get hurt."

He flushed, mouth tightening into a grim line. Before he could reply, a stocky man in stained buckskins took the youth's arm in a firm grip.

"Time to go, young sir. Your father is looking for you." He focused bloodshot eyes on me. "Apologies, madam. The young master forgets himself at times."

The stocky man dragged the protesting youth away. *Interesting.* I finished my drink, mulling over the interaction. A piece of a puzzle for another day, perhaps.

Soon after, a man matching the description I'd been given by one of my whisperers as a potential asset, slid into the now vacant seat beside me, glancing around furtively.

"Whiskey," he barked at the bartender. He was brown-haired and nondescript, easily forgotten in a crowd. But my informant had been specific. Burn scar on the right hand. This was the guy.

When he made no move to address me, I cleared my throat. "Quite the crowd tonight."

"Mmph." He gulped his whiskey without looking at me.

I tried again. "Rumor has it there's a storm coming. Bad for the ships."

His eyes darted to me then back to his drink. "If you know what's good for you, you'll stay out of it, missy. No good comes from storms."

"Depends who guides the ship."

He shook his head vehemently. "Not this time. This storm will swallow you whole."

I leaned closer, dropping my voice. "I'm searching for someone. Young women who have...vanished, in recent days. I wonder if you know where they might be."

His breathing quickened, and he tossed back the rest of his whiskey with a grimace. "No good will come of this, I'm telling you."

"Humor me."

He hesitated, eyes darting again before leaning in close. "You didn't hear it from me, but word is Lord Stanton's been...collecting again. Pretty young lasses no one will miss. The prettier, the better."

My blood turned to ice, as I pressed on with a hunch. "There's one in particular I'm looking for. Chestnut curls, green eyes. A real beauty."

His eyebrows rose in recognition. "Ah, yes. She'd catch his lordship's eye, damn sure. Saw her myself not long ago, with one of Stanton's men." His shoulders hunched with remembered fear. "Couldn't miss those eyes. Like emeralds in the sun."

Rage burned through me, hot and urgent. I had to forcibly unclench my fists. This confirmed that that sick bastard *was* targeting Amelia.

Oblivious to my reaction, the informant rambled on. "S'only a matter of time before he tires of this place for a while. Then it's off to the country estate where no one will find…"

He trailed off as I slid coins across the bar, staring intently. "The country estate. Where?"

"I've said too much already. She's as good as gone."

My fingers shot out, gripping his wrist in a vice. I caught his panicked gaze and held it.

"Tell me. Now." My voice was deadly calm.

Sweat beaded his forehead as he searched my face. Whatever he saw in my expression made him gulp. "O-outside London. Off the Dover road." He recited some rudimentary directions in a shaky voice.

I released his wrist, nodding in satisfaction as I committed the directions to memory. That was a start. I flipped another coin his way which he scrabbled for, not meeting my eyes again. He scurried away a moment later.

The night air was brisk and sobering as I stepped outside the Black Boar tavern, the boisterous voices fading behind me.

I tugged my cloak tighter against the chill, thoughts swirling from the evening's revelations.

I wound through the cobblestone streets back toward my bookshop, moving silently out of long habit. I was several blocks away when the hairs on my neck prickled with the distinct sensation of being watched. Casually, I paused as if to examine a shop window, using the glass to discreetly scan the empty street behind me. Sure enough, a large shadow peeled away from a nearby alley, keeping pace some distance behind.

My pulse quickened, but I gave no outward sign, resuming my walk at a steady pace. Could be a random footpad looking for a vulnerable mark. But my instincts said otherwise. As I turned down a narrow side street, the shadowed figure followed. Whoever he was, he moved quietly with long, sure strides. Not some common street thug then.

I cursed internally, mind racing through possibilities. One of Stanton's men, sent to intimidate me after the tavern? Or perhaps this had nothing to do with Stanton, and was related to another old adversary. Either way, leading this menacing tail back to my shop and home wasn't an option.

I turned abruptly down another alley, increasing my pace. The footsteps matched my acceleration, neither gaining nor falling behind. A professional then. Excellent. I lived for a challenge.

When the footsteps rounded the corner behind me, I was ready, pressing myself flat against the brick wall, dagger drawn. As the figure rushed past, I struck, sweeping his legs out from under him with a swift kick. He crashed to the ground with a grunt and I pinned him there neatly, dagger tip pressed to his throat. By the dim light of the moon I made out a nondescript, bearded face twisted into a scowl.

"Why are you following me?" I kept my tone low and calm.

He spat. "Unhand me, witch!"

I pressed the blade harder, drawing a pinprick of blood. "Wrong answer. Let's try again. Who sent you?"

The man's eyes widened, his bluster melting away. "I...I

don't know his name. Tall gent, fancy clothes. Paid me a fat purse to track your movements tonight."

"Where did you meet him? Describe the location."

He swallowed thickly. "Some bakeshop. Toffino's I think. Up near the square."

I committing the details to memory. That was something to go on at least.

The blade bit deeper, a crimson rivulet spilling down his neck as his face contorted in fear. With a silent curse, I retracted the blade and slammed the hilt against the man's temple, sending him slumping into unconsciousness. Hardly an elegant solution, but it would have to do.

I rifled quickly through his pockets, searching for anything that could identify me later. I did not need him tracking me down once he awoke, although any seasoned professional would know better than to pursue revenge after being bested. You live longer letting such defeats go.

Satisfied there was nothing, I dragged the man's limp form behind a pile of garbage bins. He'd wake with one hell of a headache, but he'd live. I slipped silently from the alley and merged into the night shadows.

Despite the encounter, I kept my senses alert for any other potential tails all the way back to my bookshop. At this late hour, the shop was locked up tight, just a faint glow from the back room indicating Oliver had forgotten a lamp burning again. Foolish, but lucky for me now as I slipped around to use my hidden key on the back entrance.

Inside, the place was still and peaceful. I breathed deep amidst the comforting smell of leather and parchment, letting it soothe my lingering adrenaline. No matter the dangers gathering, I always felt safe here surrounded by my books. Their stories offered useful wisdom I'd drawn on many times.

I moved silently through the shadowed rows to the back. As expected, I found dear, fussy Oliver slumped asleep at the desk, head pillowed on his arms. An open ledger was beneath him, trailing a thin line of drool. His round, pleasant face looked years younger relaxed in sleep.

I reached out gently to shake him awake. He snorted, sitting bolt upright and blinking owlishly. "Wha—Elizabeth!" He jumped to his feet, nearly toppling the chair, cheeks flushing as he dabbed at the ledger. "I must have dozed off. So sorry about that, won't happen again."

I waved off his flustered apologies with an amused smile I couldn't quite contain. "No harm done, Oliver. Though I'd avoid sleeping on the books themselves. Some of these are quite irreplaceable, you know."

"Er, right you are, miss." He tidied some already orderly piles, not quite meeting my eye.

I took pity on him them, softening my tone. "It's late. Go home and get some rest. I'll close up here." Oliver took such pride in his job, I hated embarrassing him.

"Oh, are you certain? I don't mind..."

I cut him off. "Quite. Goodnight, Oliver. See you tomorrow."

"Well, if you insist. Goodnight then, Elizabeth." He shuffled out dutifully. I waited until the door clicked softly behind him before sinking down in his vacated chair with a long sigh, letting my calm façade slip.

What a bloody mess. I dropped my head into my hands, rubbing my temples. That iron control that had served me so well all those years locked away inside myself now felt like an ill-fitting coat, scratchy and confining.

I thought I'd left it all behind. The constant suspicion, looking over my shoulder, trusting no one. Drawing blades on men in dark alleys. All necessary survival skills in my past life, but exhausting to keep up forever. I'd dared to hope those days of shadows were behind me for good.

One thing was for sure...with the return of the anxiety from my old lifestyle that I knew would inevitably take over, I was going to have to find a way to blow off steam if I had any chance of keeping my wits about me.

Chapter 3

Late the following afternoon, the bell above the door chimed as Thomas sauntered into the bookshop, the sound slicing through the cozy silence that had wrapped around me like a warm blanket. I looked up from the ledger I'd been scrutinizing, my breath catching as I took in the sight of him.

Even in the gaslight's moody glow fighting the cloud of a London rain, Thomas's bad boy charm was as potent as a heady shot of whiskey. His salt-and-pepper hair glistened like a knight's silver armour while the shadows danced across his weathered face, making him dangerously enticing. He moved like a panther stalking its prey, his coat billowing around his legs as his ice-blue eyes locked onto mine. The resulting grin was so deliciously wicked, it made my insides dance.

"Fancy seeing you here," he drawled, coming to lean casually against the counter. "I hope I'm not interrupting anything important."

I snorted, shoving the ledger aside. "Just balancing the books, which might actually be the dullest thing ever invented."

Thomas chuckled, the rich sound reverberating through me. "Well in that case, I'm happy to provide a distraction."

"Is that what you are?" I mused, cocking an eyebrow. "A distraction?"

"Among other things," he returned smoothly, holding my gaze with a heat that made my cheeks flush.

Get it together, Lizzie. I gave myself a mental shake, trying to ignore the way my pulse quickened whenever Thomas was near.

Clearing my throat, I summoned my most professional tone. "So, what treasure can I help you unearth today? We've got the latest Gothic tales fresh from Germany. Or perhaps a fascinating history of ancient Persia might tickle your fancy?"

Thomas considered for a moment. "Tempting. But I think what I'm really in the mood for is a bit of adventure." His eyes glinted mischievously. "What do you recommend?"

I pretended to think about it, tapping my fingers on the counter. "Well, I'm currently reading a tale of an ex-spy who gets pulled back into intrigue and danger that's quite thrilling."

"Brilliant," he crowed, grinning like a child with a secret stash of sweets. "Sold on your word. But first—" He reached into his coat and produced a parcel wrapped in modest brown paper. "A little something for you."

I raised an eyebrow but accepted the mystery gift. Unwrapping it, I discovered a lavish bottle of Bordeaux that probably cost more than my monthly rent. "Thomas...this is too much," I whispered, my fingers tracing the label reverently.

"Bollocks. It reminded me of you. Plus, what's the point of having a fortune if I can't use it to dazzle a stunning bookshop owner occasionally?" He winked, the scoundrel.

I laughed, shaking my head. "Well consider me thoroughly impressed. Thank you, truly. This is exquisite." I meant it—his gift showed real thoughtfulness.

We traded banter about books and the latest London gossip while I tidied up for the day. Thomas kept the conversation sparkling with his sharp wit, that had me smiling in spite of myself. The man had a silver tongue that could turn any frown upside down.

I noticed the light fading outside the shop windows. "Nearly dark," I murmured, glancing around uneasily.

Thomas, quick as a fox, picked up on my unease. "Elizabeth, is everything alright?"

I sighed, weighing how much to tell him. Thomas had a cool head and a strong moral compass. And right now, I needed all the level-headed allies I could get.

I lowered my voice. "Last night, I was followed through the streets by a someone. I've got a sneaky suspicion he didn't just want to compliment my hat. Since then I've felt...vulnerable." I clenched my jaw. Admitting that did not come naturally.

Thomas's expression darkened, his nonchalance evaporating like a ghost. "Any idea who they were or what they wanted?"

I shook my head grimly and spat out a boldfaced lie. "None. But things have felt off lately. Ominous."

Thomas nodded slowly, glancing around the shop as if seeing it through new eyes. "This place is pretty secluded at night," he remarked. "Easy place for an ambush."

My spine stiffened. "I can handle myself just fine."

He held up his hands in a placating gesture. "Of course. I just meant...perhaps you shouldn't be here alone after dark."

I bristled at the implication that I needed coddling or protecting. I'd been an intelligence operative for over a decade, dammit. But Thomas's concern seemed genuine, and the shop's isolation did leave me exposed.

Swallowing my pride, I said, "You're probably right. What did you have in mind?"

"Let's go upstairs," he suggested, his eyes sparkling with their devilish charm. "We can share that bottle of Bordeaux."

The offer was temptation itself— an intimate evening in my cozy apartment with a man who intrigued me more each day. Caution warred with curiosity.

Sensing my hesitation, Thomas attempted to soothe my fears. "I swear on my honor to behave like a perfect gent," he pledged, hand on his heart, "unless, of course, the lady specifies otherwise." His wink sent my pulse skittering again.

"Oh, you're incorrigible," I huffed, swatting his arm. But the prospect of good conversation was too enticing to resist after the isolation of recent days. "Come on then," I relented with a grin. "You've twisted my arm."

I locked the shop door and led Thomas up the narrow stairs to my apartment nestled above the store. He glanced around appreciatively as we entered the main living area, dominated by overflowing bookshelves and a crackling fireplace.

"It's quite cozy up here," Thomas remarked, shedding his coat and rolling up his sleeves as he surveyed my small kitchen.

I busied myself with candle lighting duties while Thomas played explorer in my cupboards, searching for suitable glasses.

I retrieved the bottle of Bordeaux and poured us each a glass, savoring the deep ruby hue.

"To adventure," Thomas toasted with a roguish wink, clinking his glass to mine. The wine's lush flavor burst across my tongue, warming me from the inside out. Thomas met my gaze over the rim of his glass, something unspoken passing between us. A whisper of possibility.

Our evening was a delightful dance of wit and repartee, punctuated by comfortable silences. We devoured a quick supper and polished off the wine. It was the most fun I'd had since...well, I couldn't remember when.

After helping with the cleanup, Thomas pulled a leather-bound edition of Arabian Nights from my library. "Indulge me?" he asked, a charming smile playing on his lips. "Your voice is the perfect tonic after a day of hustle and bustle."

Soon we were deep in the pages, savoring the words that I tried to make come alive with my voice. The crackling of the fireplace provided a comforting background noise as Thomas watched me from across the room, his eyes traveling over my body appreciatively.

Elizabeth," he murmured, his voice like warm honey dripping onto my skin.

I ignored him, engrossed in the story of the sultan who falls hopelessly in love. The vivid imagery painted a picture in my mind of the forbidden trysts and dangerous passion, making my heart race.

Thomas approached silently, his footsteps echoing softly against the hardwood floor. His scent - leather and musk - surrounded me, intoxicating. I felt his presence before I saw him, an electrifying prickle moving up my spine. He leaned down, his mouth hovering near my ear.

"May I?" he whispered, his breath tickling my ear.

I nodded, not trusting my voice.

He slid the book from my grasp and laid it gently on the table beside me, his warm hands trailing down my arms. I shivered at the gentle touch as he moved behind me, his body close but not touching.

He read over my shoulder, our breaths mingling in the cool air between us. We sat like that for what felt like an eternity, lost in the erotic tale of Sinbad and his various adventures. His fingers brushed against the nape of my neck, sending shivers down my spine.

"This is quite...daring," he mused, his voice a low rumble in his chest.

I nodded as desire pooled low in my stomach, my mind wrestling with the implications of what might occur if I let it.

His fingers began to trace the delicate lines of my collarbone, sending tingles down my arms.

Fuck it, I thought...wasn't I just saying I needed to find a way to blow off steam? Or was my mind just muddled from the wine and the closeness?

Then his fingers were no longer tracing – they were pulling me gently back, his lips finding the soft skin under my ear while a moan escaped me, unbidden.

He kissed his way up to my jaw, his stubble rough against my skin. "Elizabeth," he murmured, each syllable a whispered caress as his teeth grazed my earlobe and I melted into him.

Thomas slid his hands up my sides, cupping my breasts through my dress. His touch igniting a fire within me, making me ache for him.

"Tell me..." he breathed into my ear, sending shivers down my spine. "Have you ever been with someone who knew how to please you?"

I swallowed hard. "I have, but I suspect you're about to give them a run for their money."

His laughter was deep and throaty. "Flatterer," he said moving to face me. Our faces were inches apart, his intense gaze holding mine captive.

He leaned toward me, his breath sending shivers down my spine as he hooked his fingers into the ties of my gown and began to tug slowly.

The fabric loosened, parting under his gentle yet firm pull, revealing more of my flesh with each tug. He dragged the silky material all the way down to my waist, baring my corset. My heart raced as his hands traveled up my sides, fingers grazing the sensitive skin beneath my arms and over my collarbones before reaching behind me for the next set of ties.

Soon, the corset came undone, and he pushed it off, letting it fall to the floor in a puddle at our feet. It landed with a soft thud, revealing my bare breasts to his hungry eyes. With a groan, he lowered his mouth to one of them, taking a hardened nipple into his mouth and sucking gently. Pleasure shot through me, and I arched into him.

God, the feeling of his tongue circling, the rasp of his beard against my sensitive skin. I moaned softly as he teased and tasted his way down my body - his hands roaming over my ribcage, fingers dancing across my warm skin as he explored every inch.

He was taking his time, drawing out the anticipation, making sure I felt every touch, every caress, every breath he took against my skin. His hands moved lower, trailing over my abdomen and hip bones before encountering the waist of my dress again.

He pulled me from my chair and as I stood, the already untied dress fell slowly. He took my hand and stepped me out of the dress, then slowly, reverently, pulled my last layer down, finally revealing the dampness between my thighs.

My body shuddered as he teased me with his breath.

Thomas lay me on my bed, the air heavy with desire, our gasps filling the silence as he dipped low again, his warm breath fanning over my sensitive folds. His tongue flicked out to taste me, tracing circles and swirls that set my mind reeling.

I couldn't help but wriggle under the sensations. He chuckled darkly against me, the sound rumbling through my body like an earthquake. His hands left my hips to move down my thighs, pushing them apart as he knelt between them. He looked up at me then, his eyes blazing with hunger and something else I couldn't quite place. It was both terrifying and exhilarating all at once. And then he was licking, long slow strokes that sent shivers down my spine and made me see stars behind my eyelids.

"God, Elizabeth," he murmured against my moist flesh.

And then his tongue parted me once more as he spread my legs even wider.

Fuck.

A rush of sensations pummelled me, an involuntary moan escaping my lips, which only sent Thomas into overdrive, clasping my hips tighter to bring me closer to his mouth. His tongue was deft and dextrous, soft and teasing, and then it became greedy, licking harder, finding my clit and gently flicking before his lips pressed around it.

Over and over, his tongue flicked and then he sucked until I began to move my hips beneath him, the pressure building hard and fast.

But he wasn't about to let me off that easily, suddenly backing away...but only momentarily before he gifted me with a new sensation. One finger slipped inside me, a glorious, though short-lived kind of relief, my legs instinctively parting even wider, my feet finding purchase on his shoulders as he knelt before me. A second finger slipped in then, a primal groan easing out of me as he was easing in.

"Jesus fuck," I said, unable to keep the words inside.

He began to move those miracle fingers slowly, rocking ever so slightly as he did so that my feet that were planted on his shoulders began to rock with him, my hips lifting and rocking as he pulsed deeper with every thrust.

I wasn't sure how much more I could take, even as I hoped the sensations would never end, but then he hit me with the one-two punch, his mouth clamping over my clit as he continued to thrust his fingers, curling them to reach that ever-elusive—though, apparently not-so-elusive to Thomas—g-spot.

He sucked as I screamed out, bucking against him as my explosion came hard, his lips slowly, patiently, completely, coaxing every blessed wave from somewhere deep inside me.

I lay there dazed, unable to move for a minute, and Thomas stayed right where he was, allowing me to relish in the sensations as long as I needed.

When I finally stirred, his fingers slid gently out and I missed them immediately, even as he kissed my most sensitive area one last, gentle time.

"I want to be inside you," he said, his voice husky with need.

Chapter 4

Thomas pulled off his shirt, revealing his muscular form, and then the pants, along with everything else went, and I couldn't help but whimper in anticipation of having his impressive shaft inside me.

Thankfully, he didn't make me wait long, as he quickly donned protection. "Thank god for modern medicine," he said as slowly, he pushed in, sliding easily, filling me completely.

"Elizabeth," he groaned, his voice raw with desire. I matched his groan, feeling every inch of him stretching me. He began to move within me, our bodies in perfect harmony. Our skin clapped together rhythmically, creating an erotic beat that echoed in the quiet room. Each thrust sent shockwaves of pleasure through my body. I grabbed onto him tighter, losing myself in the moment...in him.

As we moved together, he leaned in once more to capture my lips in a deep, passionate kiss. Our tongues danced wildly, and I tasted the remnants of the Bordeaux, and myself, on his lips. Our hearts raced in unison, our breaths coming out in short pants as we lost ourselves in each other's embrace.

His hands roamed across my body, trailing over my curves and caressing my skin. There was something so intoxicating about being desired like this...about having someone who knew just how to touch me to send shivers down my spine. He reached down between us, finding my clit, teasing it mercilessly.

I bit my bottom lip to stifle my cries, as his other hand moved up to cradle my face, his thumb tracing circles around my jawline. His touch was both possessive and comforting.

The room filled with the sounds of our lovemaking - his

rough raspy breaths and the occasional soft moan escaping my lips. It was all utterly intoxicating.

My mind went blank as I surrendered myself fully to him.

The friction built between us, the pressure mounting...and then he stopped.

I whimpered in protest but he shushed me with another kiss. "Trust me," he whispered against my lips before adjusting his angle. His hips started to pump again, hitting a place inside me that sent me spiraling out of control.

His free hand moved to cup my breast, squeezing it gently. As he continued to thrust into me, his thumb brushed against my nipple in a slow, teasing circle that sent shockwaves of pleasure through my body. I closed my eyes and lost myself in the feeling, abandoning all thoughts except for the sensations coursing through my veins.

Finally, finally, we reached our peak together. His moans grew louder at his release, his body shuddering with force. He collapsed on top of me, kissing my neck and shoulders, nibbling gently as if he can't get enough of my taste. I clung onto him, our sweat mingling as we caught our breath together.

After a few moments, he rolled off and I looked up at him, my cheeks flushed from the heat of desire and admiration.

He smirked down at me. "Well," he chuckled, "that was certainly unexpected."

"Wasn't it though?" I managed to say between pants, my heart still racing from the afterglow.

We both leaned in for another kiss, this time slower and more tender. The taste of each other lingered on our lips as we savored the moment, not wanting to let go of the connection just yet.

The candlelight flickered across Thomas's chiseled features as we lay tangled in the sheets, our bodies intertwined in the aftermath of passion. My heart still raced from our frenzied lovemaking, my skin tingling where his hands had roamed. It had been ages since I'd let loose, casting aside my restraints to indulge in pure carnal pleasure.

Thomas traced lazy circles along my spine, his touch igniting sparks across my flesh. "Well, Miss Templeton, I'd say that was worth the wait, wouldn't you?" His eyes twinkled with mischief, his salt-and-pepper scruff accentuating the roguish grin spreading across his face.

I stretched like a cat, reveling in the delicious soreness in my muscles. "Mmm, I'd say it exceeded expectations. Although I should warn you, Mr. Callahan, I'm not in the habit of bedding every man who sidles up to my bookshop."

He chuckled, low and throaty. "Now that's a damn shame. A woman like you deserves to take her pleasures where she can find them."

Propping myself up on my elbows, I met his gaze unflinchingly. "Let's not get ahead of ourselves here. This was...nice. But I prefer to keep things simple."

Thomas studied me for a moment before giving a slow nod. "Fair enough. No strings attached it is." He leaned in, his breath hot against my ear. "But simple doesn't have to be boring. I'm always up for a repeat performance if you are."

A shiver rippled through me at his words, my body already craving more of his skilled touch. Still, I kept my tone nonchalant as I extracted myself from the tangle of sheets.

"We'll see about that. For now, I believe we could both use a drink." I slid from the bed and sauntered across the room, acutely aware of his eyes trailing over my naked form. Rummaging through a cabinet, I unearthed a bottle of aged whiskey and two glasses.

Thomas accepted the drink with an appreciative murmur, taking a slow sip as I nestled against the pillows, the amber liquid sending a trail of heat down my throat. A comfortable silence descended, the gentle crackling of the dying fire the only sound punctuating the night.

My shoulders tensed as my thoughts drifted back to reality, the peaceful illusion shattered by memories of the day's events. The fear in that girl's eyes....

Lord knows I tried to leave that world behind, but it seems

trouble has a way of finding me.

Thomas's fingers grazed my arm, his touch gentle. "That look in your eyes…something's bothering you."

I hesitated, warring with myself. Thomas was still such an enigma in many ways. Could I trust him with the truth?

Sensing my reluctance, he squeezed my shoulder. "Whatever you say won't leave this room. But keeping it bottled up won't help either."

Letting out a measured breath, I turned to meet his gaze. "You're not wrong. It's just…I'm used to handling things on my own."

"No one can go it alone forever," he said softly. "Even you need to let someone in now and then."

The simple truth of his words pierced my defenses. If I was going to move forward, I couldn't keep clinging to the shadows of my past.

Haltingly at first, then with increasing conviction, I opened up about the events of the past few days. The purse snatching, the encounter with the terrified girl, the feeling of unseen eyes tracking my movements.

Thomas listened intently, his sharp eyes assessing. When I finally fell silent, he let out a low whistle. "Sounds like you've landed yourself in deep waters. What are you going to do?"

I raked a hand through my hair, the carefree atmosphere from earlier completely dissipated. "Honestly? I haven't got a damn clue. Getting involved will only lead to trouble, but I can't pretend I didn't see what I saw. That girl needs help, and she's not the only one."

"Stanton," Thomas muttered darkly. At my sharp look, he grimaced. "You're not the only one who's been hearing things. Rumors carry on the wind, whispers in the dark about those in power and what they'll do to keep it." He turned to stare into the fire, his jaw taut. "If even half of what they say is true…"

I shivered despite the lingering heat, my mind churning through the implications. Lord Stanton headed one of the most influential families in the city. His philanthropy and status gave him access to the upper echelons of society.

"Corruption is like cancer," I said finally. "Left unchecked, it spreads insidiously until the whole bloody system is rotted through. I've seen it happen in other countries, and the tyranny that results." I shook my head bitterly. "Trouble is coming, whether I go looking for it or not."

Thomas nodded, shadows flickering across his face. "In my experience, it's better to be the one holding the element of surprise. Fortune favors the bold, as they say."

I almost smiled at that. Thomas and his bloody reckless philosophies. But looking at him then, I felt something shift between us. No matter how casual our affair, we were two people aware that we stood upon a crumbling precipice, faced with a choice that could change everything.

I stared at our joined hands, conflicted emotions swirling within me. "Getting close to people...it never ends well. Not in my experience." I exhaled shakily. "If anything happened to her...."

"You can't blame yourself for the actions of villains," Thomas said firmly. "Whatever comes, we'll face it on our feet, not on our knees. I'm with you, Elizabeth."

My breath caught at the intensity in those sea-blue eyes. I wasn't used to having someone stand with me in the face of darkness. It was daunting, but also exhilarating. Together, maybe we could achieve what neither of us could manage alone.

I gave his hand a swift squeeze before extricating myself from the sheets once more. We had planning to do.

Over glasses of whiskey, our conversation turned strategic. We discussed gathering intelligence on Stanton's holdings and connections, reaching out to the street kids and drifters whose eyes and ears permeated every corner of London.

We plotted ways to place informants among Stanton's vast network of businesses, taverns, and residences. The thrill of the hunt woke my senses, my mind humming as it had in years past. I found myself relaxing into the familiar role of spymaster, with Thomas proving an adept player himself.

"We'll need secure methods for exchanging information," he mused, idly swirling the amber liquid in his glass. "I have a few useful contacts on the less savory side of the law." His lips quirked wryly when I shot him a look. "Let's just say I have some experience in subterfuge."

I cocked a brow, filing away that intriguing bit of knowledge for later consideration. "My bookshop is central and discreet. We can do our planning here."

Thomas nodded thoughtfully. "I can reach out to some of the, shall we say, less constrained lads who frequent the tavern near the docks."

My pulse quickened as the plan took shape. This was the world I knew best, the chess match of wits and danger. If we played it right, we just might pull it off.

Thomas raised his glass. "To rebel alliances and new beginnings."

Chapter 5

The godawful woolen shawl itched like a bitch as I disembarked from the carriage, the frigid London air trying its damnedest to penetrate the cloak. I pulled the fabric tighter, ensuring my face remained concealed in shadow. The last thing I needed was some pickled lush recognizing me as I slithered through the East End's grimy arteries. The last thing I needed was some pickled lush recognizing me as I slithered through the East End's grimy arteries.

The cobblestones shimmered under the lamplight, slick with rain and god-knows-what-else. I picked my way carefully, avoiding the deeper puddles and piles of nameless debris.

The neighborhood was still awake despite the late hour, with raucous laughter and shouting spilling from the ramshackle buildings lining the cramped alleyways. A boozy pair clung onto each other for dear life, belting out a tune that could make a banshee wince. A scraggly alley cat gave me the stink eye, ready to flee at the first sign of trouble.

I kept my stride measured but purposeful, navigating the maze of streets from memory. The Feisty Rat – a dingy excuse for a pub – was within spitting distance. As I walked, my mind turned to Amelia who had stumbled into danger through no fault of her own, very different from what I was up to in that moment. When she'd shown up at my doorstep, my heart had shattered. That bastard Stanton would pay for what he'd done. But first, I had a mission to accomplish – getting the juicy intel from my old 'friend', Scratch.

The Feisty Rat loomed out of the murk, leaning against its neighbors like a drunk too sozzled to stand. Its grimy windows gazed onto the street like dull eyes, while mold and mildew feasted on its underbelly. A rickety wooden sign creaked in the wind, inviting as a hangman's noose. But Scratch's instructions had been clear. This was the place.

Tension coiled in my gut as I neared the entrance. This was no fancy-shmancy London ballroom - one wrong move could end poorly. Fortunately, I wasn't some helpless waif. These streets held no surprises for someone with my history.

I took a deep breath and plunged into the chaos.

The tavern hit me like a slap to the face. A cacophony of sound and smells assaulted me, the place swarming with every low-life and ne'er-do-well London had to offer. I blinked against the smoky haze, the din of scheming, swearing, and swigging patrons swirled around me. Serving girls bobbed and weaved, deftly avoiding the groping hands and lewd proposals. In a dim corner, a fiddle player sawed away, his music barely audible above the ruckus.

I jostled my way through the crowd, eliciting curses and lewd commentary which I pointedly ignored. My woolen shawl kept my face obscured, and I had taken care to hunch my shoulders and shuffle my gait, disappearing into the anonymity of the rural peasant I was pretending to be.

A grimy cloud of tobacco smoke drifted across my path as I squeezed past a rowdy dice game. One burly dockworker slammed his fist down in disgust at a losing roll, upending a tankard of ale in the process. I deftly side-stepped the wash of stale liquid, pressing onward.

The cacophony faded to a dull murmur as I reached the relative privacy of the tavern's rear corner. Away from the volatile energy of the crowd, this space felt almost serene, a secluded little island filled with hazy golden light. A single rickety table occupied the corner of the room, sporting a guttering tallow candle that threw dancing shadows across the dingy walls. Two chairs were pushed neatly against its edges.

Right on cue, a hulking figure extricated itself from the gloom, the floorboards creaking in protest under the considerable weight as Scratch materialized before me. His nickname was well earned – a jagged scar carved its way down his cheek, so prominent it was visible even under the shadow of his hat. Beneath the layers of grime and stubble, intelligent eyes peered out, scanning me up and down.

Wordlessly, Scratch settled into one of the rickety chairs, gesturing for me to follow suit. I slid onto the seat across, muscles taut and ready for action. The plan was simple: pretend we didn't know each other.

"Apologies, but I don't believe I caught your name?"

Scratch's mouth quirked in fleeting amusement. "No names needed for our purposes. I take it you're the one I was told to expect?" His voice emerged as a low rumble, gravelly with disuse.

I gave a timid nod. "Come to play a friendly game, as I was instructed. Though I confess, I don't have much experience with city folk and their ways." I lowered my eyes, affecting meekness.

Scratch leaned back in his seat, wood groaning under the shift of his bulk. "No worries," he replied, the wood groaning under his weight. "My man, Slippery Jack, will show you the ropes."

As if on cue, a wiry, pockmarked man emerged from a darkened alcove, a deck of cards held loosely in his hands. Everything about him seemed fluid and serpentine, from his lanky build to the oily gleam of his hair. His grin revealed several missing teeth. Lovely.

"Why don't we make this game more interestin' for all, eh?" the man—Slippery Jack—said. "If you win, I'll provide you with the information you came here seeking. But if you lose..." His smile turned predatory. "Me and my men will have to find our fun elsewhere." He licked his lips and took a long, meandering gaze down the length of me. "Do we have a deal?"

I bit my lip and gave what I hoped passed for a nervous nod. Inside, however, I was as excited as a peacock in a mirror shop.

Slippery Jack slid a chair over with surprising grace, immediately setting to shuffling the cards in complex patterns.

His bony fingers moved hypnotically through the deck as he appraised me with a sly smirk. This guy clearly got off on swindling. I plastered my face with the best "I don't know what I'm doing" look that I could muster and studied his sleights of hand. His movements were quick, almost imperceptible – just what you'd expect from a con artist. I'd have to be as careful as a virgin in a brothel.

Like vultures to a carcass, the tavern's most unappealing patrons swarmed our table, betting half their life's savings on this twisted game of poker. I affected an air of bewildered innocence, playing my part of the country novice to perfection. The first few hands I lost spectacularly, fumbling the cards and eliciting howls of laughter from the onlookers. With each round, I hesitantly raised the stakes, emboldening Jack. His greed would be his downfall.

A few hands in, I started to see the method behind Jack's madness. A flick of the wrist here, a kick under the table there, all designed to distract and deceive. Clever tactics, but predictable once you knew what to look for. I started employing deliberate clumsiness to disguise my own trickery, using my sleeve to hide cards and feigning distracting noises at opportune times. Slowly but surely, the game began to tilt in my favor.

The laughter around the table died down as I rallied, winning hand after hand. Jack's grin faded, his movements becoming more agitated. A sheen of sweat glinted on his brow. The cards blurred as they danced between our fingers, our eyes locked in subtle combat. An ace here, a replacement card there, sleight of hand and misdirection battling through the turns. The crowd held its breath, transfixed by the display of skill.

At long last, I lay my final hand down with flourish – a perfect king's set. Jack froze, cards hovering limply in his grip. His mirth was gone, replaced by a look of pure shock. I leaned back and held his gaze evenly, letting the barest hint of a smile grace my lips.

The tavern exploded into chaos as I claimed victory over Slippery Jack. Patrons shouted and shoved, coins exchanging hands as bets were furiously settled. Jack stared at the cards laying accusingly on the table, his face contorting through emotions ranging from disbelief to anger. For a moment, I thought he might lunge across the table in a desperate bid to reclaim his dignity. But one subtle hand motion from Scratch kept him rooted in place, impotent rage burning in his eyes.

I rose calmly from my seat, brushing dust from my cloak. The thrill of my triumph sang in my veins, but I kept my features schooled in a mask of humble gratitude. Scratch stood as well, unfolding from his chair like a bear rising on its hind legs. He towered over me, yet I refused to let intimidation cow me. I had won, now it was time to collect my prize.

Jack reached into his grimy overcoat. I tensed, prepared for anything. His hand emerged clutching a small envelope, sealed in red wax. He handed it over wordlessly. I wasted no time in secreting it within my own garments, letting the coarse fabric once more obscure the prize from sight. If Scratch could be trusted—a big if—it contained everything I needed to begin unraveling Lord Stanton's sprawling web of corruption.

"A pleasure doing business with you." I inclined my head politely to Slippery Jack, then Scratch. He merely grunted in reply, already turning away dismissively. The transaction was concluded. I had no desire to linger in this den of thieves a moment longer.

The crowd parted reluctantly as I slipped through the rowdy tavern. The fetid air felt sweeter once I pushed my way outside, leaving the din of The Feisty Rat behind. Cool, misty air enveloped me, welcome after the reek of the pub.

I turned my steps toward the darkened street, footsteps echoing on damp cobblestones.

I had only walked a few yards before the hairs on the back of my neck prickled with warning. I was being followed. Rather than panic or quicken my stride, I maintained an easy, measured pace, listening intently. There - the faint scrape of leather on stone, the methodical footsteps of men experienced in stealth. Two sets, if I wasn't mistaken. Jack's men, no doubt, sent to retrieve what I'd taken. That envelope was truly more valuable than I'd realized if he was willing to risk ambushing me in the open street. No matter. I hadn't survived this long through luck alone.

At the next narrow side passage, I darted left, my soft-soled boots granting speed and silence. The footsteps behind me broke into a run, no longer bothering with stealth. I let myself smile, wild energy coursing through my limbs. The hunt was on. I knew these streets like the back of my hand. My pursuers, underestimating me because of my gender and size, would soon realize their error.

The thrill of the chase sang in my veins as I plunged into the maze of alleyways twisting behind the taverns and decrepit buildings. I led my pursuers on a merry chase, using every trick and tactic I'd honed over long years of practice. An unlocked door provided momentary respite to circle back and reverse course. A gracefully scaled wall took me over a heap of trash and out of sight. I darted left, then right, through crumbling archways and around choked courtyards, the footsteps dogging me every step of the way.

Despite the immediate peril, I felt alive, every sense operating on razor's edge. My skills had not dulled despite my time away from the field. I still possessed the speed, the instinctual ability to read my environment and use it to my advantage. Perhaps, despite my fears, I was still capable of making a difference again.

The footsteps slowed, then stopped, as my pursuers lost themselves in the maze while I slipped away into the night. The thrill still thrummed in my chest as I slowed my pace, catching my breath. But along with exhilaration came chilling certainty - I was embroiled in something far darker than I had realized. Lord Stanton's influence was far reaching, even here, in the darkest corners of London's underworld. But I wasn't scared. No, I was angry. The envelope crinkled in my pocket, full of evidence against him. The hunt was on, and I was the hunter.

Chapter 6

I arrived at Thomas's impressive townhouse, the clicking of my heels against the marble floor announcing my presence in the grand foyer. As I glanced up at the chandelier, a monstrous thing that probably had its own gravitational pull, I felt like a fish out of water. This level of opulence was so unlike my own modest bookshop, and being surrounded by such finery made me painfully aware of how out of my element I was.

But I shook off the feeling as Thomas emerged at the top of the grand staircase.

"Elizabeth! So glad you could make it," he called out, making his way down the stairs with an easy grace.

I offered him a tight smile. "Of course. We have important business to discuss."

Thomas nodded, his smile fading slightly at my terse tone. "Right you are. But first, let me give you the grand tour. I don't often have such lovely company."

And so, off we trotted, deeper into the labyrinth of luxury. The foyer gave way to a sitting room that looked like a Victorian library had a love child with a Persian boudoir. Plush velvet chairs were arranged around an intricate rug, upon which sat an antique tea table. Crystal decanters glinted in the afternoon sunlight that streamed in through the bay windows.

"This is the east wing sitting room," Thomas explained. "It's one of my favorite spots in the house. Plenty of reading material, as you can see."

I drifted over to the nearest shelf, my eyes scanning the titles. Most were rare first editions and ancient philosophical texts. My fingers itched to pull one off the shelf and flip through its pages, but I resisted the urge.

"Quite the collection," I remarked.

He beamed, clearly pleased. "I thought you might approve. Shall we continue?"

We ventured through a warren of hallways and parlors, each more resplendent than the last. Thomas prattled on about the history of various tapestries and paintings, and I pretended to give a damn, all the while itching to get down to business.

Yet despite myself, I was impressed by the sheer magnitude of the townhouse. As we climbed a winding staircase, I paused to catch my breath, discreetly pressing a hand against my corseted ribs.

"Quite the climb," I joked weakly.

Thomas paused on the landing above me. "Ah yes, do watch your step. Wouldn't want you toppling backwards down the stairs."

His grin told me he was joking, but I still clung onto the banister like it was my lifeline. The last thing I needed was to break my neck traversing this bloody house.

At the top floor, we entered another library, this one far larger than the last. Floor to ceiling bookshelves lined the walls, accessed by rolling ladders attached to iron rails. In the center of the room sat a massive oak desk cluttered with papers and strange artifacts - likely some of Thomas's antique collecting finds.

My vertigo kicked into high gear as I peered out the window, the view so high up it made my head spin. I inhaled sharply and took a step back, pressing myself against a sturdy bookshelf.

Thomas noticed my discomfort. "Not fond of heights I take it?"

"Not particularly," I admitted with a self-deprecating laugh, trying to mask my dizziness. "Although the view is quite impressive."

Gazing out, I could see clear across the city to the clockface of Big Ben rising from the Houses of Parliament. But still, I kept my back firmly planted against the shelves as I peered.

As I ventured further into the room, Thomas pointed out a painting of a scholar who bore a striking resemblance to him.

"That's Henry Callahan, my great-grandfather" Thomas explained. "He was an avid collector and academic, just like me. Spent half his fortune gathering rare texts and artifacts. This house is his legacy."

I studied the painting more closely, noting the striking resemblance between this ancestor and Thomas himself. The same intelligent gleam in the eyes, the same thirst for knowledge.

"He left quite the legacy indeed," I murmured.

Thomas beamed with pride. But after a moment, his smile faded.

"Shall we adjourn to the drawing room? I believe we have urgent matters to discuss."

I nodded, relief flooding through me. "Yes, let's get down to business."

The grand drawing room was on the first floor, forcing a descent down the winding staircase. As Thomas swept aside the heavy velvet curtains, sunlight streamed into the room, gleaming off the polished surfaces of antique furnishings.

I wasted no time in unfurling the large intelligence map I'd brought, onto the expansive and well-loved table, already filled with pin holes. As I began marking locations with colored pins, Thomas hovered nearby, observing my efforts.

"Well, you certainly don't dally about," he remarked.

I didn't glance up from my work. "We have a sprawling criminal network to dismantle. No time to waste on pleasantries."

"Right you are."

Yet I could hear a trace of annoyance in Thomas's tone. I realized my curt manner probably seemed rude after he'd given me a thorough tour of his home. But I'd never been one for small talk or social graces. I needed action, momentum, progress.

Oblivious to my inner musings, Thomas continued watching me work, stroking his bearded chin thoughtfully.

"You know, you never did explain how you gathered all this intelligence so quickly," he mused.

I remained focused on the map, avoiding his gaze. "I have my sources."

"Indeed? And might I inquire as to the identity of these sources?"

At this, I did meet his eyes, my expression guarded. "I can't divulge that information, Thomas."

He held my gaze steadily. "Can't? Or won't?"

I crossed my arms. "And what exactly is that supposed to mean?"

Thomas sighed, running a hand through his hair. "Forgive me Elizabeth, I didn't mean to imply any dishonesty on your part. I know you would never compromise your integrity, nor mine. I suppose I am just…concerned about the risks you might be taking to acquire such intelligence."

I bristled at the insinuation that I couldn't handle myself. Hadn't I proven my skills time and time again? But before I could spit out a retort, Thomas raised his hands in supplication.

"Peace, Elizabeth. I know you are more than capable. I only want for you to be safe." His expression softened into one of sincerity. "I care about what happens to you."

My defensive anger dissipated at his words. Thomas only had my well-being at heart. But I wasn't some fragile creature in need of coddling.

I stepped closer, placing a hand on his chest. Through the fine linen of his shirt, I could feel the steady thrum of his heart.

"Your concern is duly noted," I murmured, gazing up at him. "But you know I can handle myself."

Thomas swallowed, his throat bobbing. Our faces were just inches apart. "Of course. I did not mean to imply otherwise." His voice had dropped an octave lower, rough with desire. It sent a pleasant shiver up my spine.

"See that you remember it," I whispered before closing the remaining distance between us.

The kiss obliterated all thoughts of maps and criminal

empires. Thomas responded ardently, his strong hands coming up to grip my waist, pulling our bodies flush together. I tangled my fingers in his silver-streaked hair, deepening the kiss. We stumbled backwards until my hips collided with the edge of the heavy oak table.

I broke away, gasping. "We have work to do."

Thomas nuzzled my neck. "It can wait."

His warm breath against my throat weakened my resolve. I tried half-heartedly to push him away.

"Thomas, the map..."

His hands were busy unbuttoning my blouse, his callused thumbs brushing the swells of my breasts.

"Five more minutes," he implored, his voice rough with need.

My body thrummed with desire, my mind growing pleasantly hazy. What harm could five more minutes do?

I relaxed into his embrace, the responsibilities of the day briefly forgotten as our passion carried us away. With practiced fingers, I loosened the tie of Thomas's trousers, taking him in hand. He groaned, the sound sending fresh heat pooling between my legs.

In swift motions, Thomas rid me of my blouse and skirt until I stood before him in only my corset and silk slip. The air felt cool against my exposed skin. I shivered, nipples hardening.

Thomas paused to appreciate the view, his smoldering gaze devouring the whole of me.

"Please, let me have all of you," he said, gentlemanly as ever.

"Oh, for fuck's sake, yes already," I said breathlessly, allowing him to guide me down onto the soft rug in front of the fireplace. The flames cast a warm glow over our entwined bodies as we came together.

Thomas trailed hot, open-mouthed kisses down my neck and across my breasts, eliciting soft gasps and moans. I arched into his touch, already slick with desire. His fingers danced along the inside of my thighs, teasing ever closer to where I ached for him.

"Please, Thomas," I pleaded.

With a roguish grin, his fingers finally found my center, stroking deftly as my hips bucked against him. He watched my face intently as he played my body like a well-tuned instrument, bringing me to the brink with practiced skill.

Just as I neared my peak, he shifted above me, our gazes locking, and without breaking eye contact, he entered me in one smooth motion. I cried out, wrapping my legs around his hips as he filled me.

Suddenly, I pushed him back, taking control as we flipped and I straddled him, riding him wildly, roughly as I gasped his name, feeling the thundering of his heart beneath me. His strong arms wrapped around me, holding onto me as if he never wanted to let go. All thoughts of maps and criminals faded away as we lost ourselves in passion's sweet rhythm.

I came in a blaze of sensation, shuddering and clenching around him. Moments later his pace grew erratic as he found his own release. I held him close, our hearts thundering in tandem as we caught our breath.

Eventually we parted and Thomas pulled me against his side. I pillowed my head on his chest, listening to his heart rate slow.

"Well done, darling," he whispered, his voice filled with awe.

I let out a low chuckle. "Why thank you, kind sir," I replied with a satisfied smirk.

But the languid afterglow could not last forever. Too soon, the pressing matters of the day began to creep back into my mind, breaking the spell of our shared passion.

With no small amount of regret, I slowly disentangled from Thomas's embrace and began gathering my discarded clothing. He watched with hooded eyes as I made myself presentable once more, sealing away the flushed, wanton creature I became in his arms.

When I was once again buttoned, tucked and laced, I smoothed my hair and turned my attention back to the map strewn across the table. Thomas came up behind me, winding his arms around my waist and nuzzling the sensitive spot beneath my ear.

"Must we return to business so soon?" His voice was a low rumble that made my already weak knees threaten to buckle.

With effort, I twisted out of his embrace. "I'm afraid so. Much to be done."

Thomas sighed but nodded, lacing his own trousers back up. "You're right, of course. What's our next move?"

I appreciated his willingness to set aside pleasure for the task at hand. As much as our passion ignited like wildfire, we had to keep the flames at bay when necessity called.

Returning my focus to the map, I scanned the web of locations, my finger trailing the network of red strings I had pinned. Towards the east, an intersection of several strings caught my eye. I tapped it thoughtfully.

"Here. This property on Cheshire Street seems to be a hub of activity. We should start our surveillance there."

Thomas peered at the spot I indicated, stroking his beard. "Hmm, yes. I believe that location is owned by a shipping company connected to Stanton's enterprise. Well spotted."

I allowed myself a small smile at his praise. We were back in our element - strategizing, scrutinizing, preparing to take action. The machinery of our minds whirred to life, two sets of keen intellects working in tandem towards one purpose. For now, the map was our singular focus.

Later, when the city's pulse quieted, our minds could turn again to more pleasurable pursuits. But duty called, and we answered readily. The coming battles would require our full faculties and cunning.

So for the present, we applied ourselves wholly to the sprawling map, searching for the loose threads we would carefully pull to unravel Stanton's web of villainy. All else would have to wait.

Chapter 7

The frosty air crept up my skirt like a naughty schoolboy as I lurked in the shadows across from a most unremarkable building on Cheshire Street. Potentially a thread in the spiderweb of Lord Stanton's crooked empire, it could hold the golden ticket to blowing his repugnant crime ring wide open. Or at least I fucking hoped so.

Beside me, Thomas was doing a dance to keep his toes from freezing off. "Again, why are we turning into icicles watching an empty haunted building at god-awful o'clock?"

I shot him a look that was almost as icy as our surroundings. "We're playing detective, obviously. If we can spot any of Stanton's minions or their delivery routes, we might just have enough to crush his operation."

Thomas grumbled something that sounded like "I'd rather be in a warm bed", but he knew as well as I did that this was the only way to get what we needed. Stakeouts were about as glamorous as a chamber pot, but they often led to catching the bad guys with their trousers down.

The wait was misery, time crawling along like a geriatric tortoise as the chill worked its way into my marrow. I shot mental daggers at the building, willing it to give up its secrets. But the street was as quiet as a mouse fart, with only the echo of hooves on cobblestone in the distance piercing the heavy silence.

My thoughts wandered to Amelia, the urgency of finding an end to her torture pressed down on me like a physical weight. If my meddling made things worse... I shook off the thought. Guilt was a slippery slope, and I was already too familiar with its treacherous terrain.

To distract myself, I glanced over at Thomas again. I envied how at ease he seemed, his eyes calmly scanning our surroundings. He was a riddle wrapped in an enigma, wrapped in a really good-looking package. I studied his profile in the glow of the gas lamps. His salt-and-pepper hair shone silver, giving him a distinguished air that I knew concealed a recklessness and hunger for adventure. His piercing eyes held a world of secrets.

Thomas turned his head slightly, catching me studying him. One corner of his mouth turned up.

"See something intriguing?" His voice held a hint of playful suggestiveness that brought an involuntary flush to my cheeks.

"Don't flatter yourself," I whispered sharply. "I was merely assessing your alertness."

"Sure you were." His voice was dripping with self-satisfaction, which was annoying but also weirdly arousing. Damn the man, why must he be so vexing and attractive all at once?

I cleared my throat and returned my gaze to the silent building. I needed to focus. Amelia's life was on the line, along with countless others ensnared in Stanton's web. I couldn't afford to get distracted by thoughts of Thomas's muscly arms or those soft lips of his...

A scrape of movement at the alley's mouth jolted me sharply back to the present. I placed my hand on Thomas's arm in warning as a figure emerged from the darkness, the tap of his boots on stone strangely loud in the muffled night.

But as the figure approached, the face that came into view was so utterly unexpected that I had to stifle a gasp. But there was no mistaking that lanky frame, the nervous flitting of the eyes under the tattered brim of his hat. Slippery Jack, the cheat I'd fleeced at cards. What the hell was he doing here?

He looked as comfortable as a cat in a bath as he scurried toward us.

Jack fidgeted like a kid who needed a piss, keeping one eye on the silent warehouse. The wind picked up, rustling the debris in the alley and sending a chill down my spine that had nothing to do with the cold. I didn't like the way this was going. Jack was clearly on edge, which made him unpredictable and dangerous.

Before I could respond, Thomas stepped forward, placing himself bodily between us in an unexpectedly protective gesture. "State your business and shuffle off," he said curtly to Jack.

"I didn't come to chat with you, pal," Jack shot back. "I need to talk to the lady."

"Then speak," I said, putting a hand on Thomas's shoulder to keep him from starting a brawl. Jack's eyes darted to follow my movement, noting it with interest.

With a final wary glance at Thomas, Jack turned his attention back to me. "I have information for you about what's going on in there tonight." He jerked his head toward the warehouse. "But we need to discuss it somewhere more private."

My pulse quickened, but I kept my face carefully blank. The intel Jack offered could be invaluable, and this might be my only chance to discover the details of Stanton's operation.

But Thomas shifted uneasily beside me. "It's rather late for a social call," his voice as frosty as a snowman's balls.

My heart pounded fiercely, but I kept my face as blank as an unwritten novel. I could only assume Slippery Jack was offering up a juicy piece of intel that could crack Stanton's operation wide open. Unfortunately, he could also expose my past in the process. Clearly, he knew more about me now than he did the other night.

I'd spent years crafting my unassuming identity as a bookshop owner, burying memories of my former life as an operative trained in subterfuge and combat.

Slippery Jack's eyes glowed with a devilish mix of greed and revenge. I began to wonder if he really was looking to hawk his knowledge to the highest bidder, or was he still nursing a bruised ego from me wiping the floor with him at the poker table? Hell if I knew. But with Amelia's fate hanging in the balance, I was willing to risk almost anything.

I locked eyes with Jack, a silent agreement passing between us. Like it or not, we were now partners in crime on this twisted path. There was no backing out now.

Jack moved ahead of me, pausing to ensure I follow. As I trailed him into the mist-shrouded London night, I felt Thomas's eyes boring into my back, his handsome face no doubt creased in concern. But my past was a secret I was not ready share, not even with Thomas. Maybe especially with Thomas.

A few blocks later, a small group of drunks were getting handsy with a woman dressed for nightwork, no doubt to attract customers of the male variety. But it was clear she wasn't interested in the kind of attention she was getting, their intentions unmistakably malicious.

"Get off me, you swine!" she hollered, struggling against an overly amorous bastard.

Thomas's attention was drawn.

Without a moment's hesitation, Thomas rushed to her aid. "Touch her again and it'll be the last thing you do!" he roared. His broad shoulders and determined gaze were enough to give the ruffians pause.

Seizing the opportunity, I shot Jack a meaningful glance and, with a pang of guilt, abandoned Thomas to his heroic endeavors.

Jack set a brisk pace along the slick cobblestones, leading me down alleyways toward the murky Thames. The scent of brine and dead fish assailed my nostrils while seagulls screamed overhead, diving for discarded scraps. Ghostly ships rocked at anchor, their masts creaking and groaning. By day this waterfront bustled with sailors and merchants from around the world, but now it slumbered uneasily, as if hiding secrets.

A sense of unease washed over me. Something was off. Jack stood a few steps ahead, a shadowy figure in the fog. Every instinct screamed that it was a trap, but for Amelia's sake, I had no choice but to walk right into it.

With measured steps I continued along the weathered docks, senses primed for the slightest hint of movement. Ahead,

Jack's form solidified out of the gloom. And he was not alone. Sinister shapes fanned out around him, burly men with assorted bludgeoning tools and knives.

So, the dickwad did have revenge on his mind after all. How disappointing.

I counted six in total as they spread out, hemming me in against the water's edge. Rough men by the look of it, dockworkers and sailors no doubt drawn from the cellars and gambling halls that Jack frequented. Their heavy shoulders and calloused hands spoke of hard lives filled with violence. Exactly the kind of brutes who believed a woman, even one like me, was easy prey.

"Evening gentlemen," I said brightly, shifting my stance to balance my weight. I flexed my wrists. "Out for a leisurely stroll?"

Low laughter rumbled around me, more mocking than mirthful. Jack stepped forward, his lips splitting into a gap-toothed grin.

"Think you're all high and mighty, do ya?" he spat. "Let's see how you like being put in your place."

His men pressed in closer, reeking of gin and ill-intent. An amused glint touched my eyes. The fools had no idea who they're dealing with.

"Oh Jack, if you desire etiquette lessons, you've come to the right woman," I replied, letting my posture relax into a deceptive casualness. "Though I should warn you, I was always a strict instructor."

Jack's grin evaporated. With a guttural snarl, he lunged forward, arms spread wide to grab me. Exactly as I expected. I twisted nimbly aside, his fingers clutching empty air. His momentum carried him stumbling past to splash down on his ass in a puddle.

Howls of laughter rose from his men as their leader spluttered indignantly. I almost felt pity for the oaf. Almost. I couldn't resist a small jab.

"First lesson – mind your footing."

Jack's face purpled with rage, his dignity bruised even more than his ego. He surged to his feet, all humor gone.

"I'll make you eat your words, you cheeky wench!" he snarled, flailing about like a child throwing a tantrum.

He came at me again, fists swinging wildly. I danced around his sloppy swings with ease, his movements as predictable as a two-penny horoscope. After facing far deadlier adversaries over the years, Jack was little more than an annoyance. But I had to end it quickly, before his wounded pride turned lethal.

As Jack staggered past again, I delivered a swift kidney punch followed by a leg sweep. He crashed down hard, the air exploding from his lungs. I pinned his arm in a brutal lock, wringing out a strangled yelp.

"Lesson two, Jack," I whispered, all sweet and sugary. "Never lose your temper in a fight."

Jack wisely went limp, wheezing. I released him and rose smoothly, turning to face his slack-jawed men. Their earlier amusement had vanished. Now they watched me with baleful glares, fingering their weapons.

I acknowledged them, adrenaline singing through my veins. "Come now gentlemen. This need not end in more bruises. Just walk away and we'll forget this unfortunate incident."

For a heartbeat, indecision held them in place. But egos bruise as easily as flesh. With a collective growl, they lunged at me.

Bless their stupid hearts.

I exploded into motion, years of training taking over. My hidden blade, tucked neatly in my skirt, deflected a jagged shiv while my boot met the ribs of a second thug. He doubled over just in time to receive my elbow as a parting gift. Down he went.

Another grabbed at my collar. I seized his wrist and pulled, using his own momentum to flip him head over heels into the harbor. The splash was most satisfying.

The remaining goons circled me cautiously, their united front falling apart under the weight of my expertise. I turned slowly, my gaze sweeping over them. Most of them looked ready to hightail it out of there rather than face my blade. But the biggest one still had some fight left in him. He roared and lunged, swinging a pipe with the intention of cracking my skull open.

Almost lazily, I sidestepped, sliced his wrist, stripped the pipe from his suddenly nerveless fingers, and swept his legs out. He hit the ground like a sack of potatoes, the wind knocked out of him. The pipe now rested lightly against his neck.

Our eyes met.

"Class dismissed," I murmured.

He gulped and nodded frantically, his good hand raised in submission. I stepped back, leaving him there like yesterday's news. Sometimes, mercy was the most potent poison.

Meanwhile, Jack was stirring, struggling to his feet, wiping a concoction of blood and grime from his chin. His beady eyes glared at me, a mix of newfound respect and unabated hatred. I held his gaze until he looked away.

"This ain't over wench," he growled, but the words lacked conviction. We both knew he was beaten. Without another word, Jack turned and limped away, his men trailing him with bowed heads and wounded pride. I watched until the fog swallowed them before finally allowing myself to breathe.

"Quite a show." The unexpected voice almost made me jump. My blade snapped up reflexively as I pivoted, lowering as I recognized the speaker.

"Oh hey, Thomas," was all I could manage.

Chapter 8

My breath caught in my throat as Thomas turned to look at me, a knowing glint in his eye. I braced for the inevitable questions. How did a simple bookshop owner like myself possess such fighting skills? Why did I move with the fluidity of a trained killer?

Questions I couldn't easily answer. Secrets I'd hoped to keep buried along with the ghosts of my past.

But Thomas just cocked one eyebrow and gave me a crooked smirk. "Well, well," he drawled. "Aren't you full of surprises, Miss Elizabeth."

I stared back mutely, heart hammering. I'd grown accustomed to hiding behind my assumed identity, never letting anyone glimpse the woman beneath the facade. The woman who could kill as easily as most ladies sipped afternoon tea.

Yet perhaps it was time to take a risk. Thomas had proven himself trustworthy so far, and I was short on allies. If I was going to take down Stanton's empire, we'd already determined I couldn't do it alone.

"Surprises indeed," I murmured back cryptically, still hesitant to reveal too much too quickly. "Though I assure you, dear Thomas, everything I do has purpose."

He stepped closer, blue eyes glittering. "Oh I don't doubt that. A woman like you clearly doesn't waste movements. And you, my dear, move like a predator."

My hackles rose at his insinuation, but I forced myself to relax. Thomas meant no offense. And truly, he wasn't wrong. There was blood on my hands despite my current facade as a bookish shopkeeper. More than he could likely imagine.

Perhaps it was that realization that spurred me forward. That nagging thought that even if he knew the truth, Thomas could handle it. Some men would balk at the notion of a woman with my sordid past. But Thomas was...different.

"Very perceptive," I said softly. "I thought I'd been careful, keeping up appearances. But clearly little escapes your notice."

He inclined his head. "Most people see only what they expect to see. But I've learned to look deeper." His eyes traveled the length of my body meaningfully. "And you, Elizabeth, are far deeper than you let on."

A shiver of anticipation ran through me at his words. He wasn't wrong. Beneath the layers of respectability, I was a coiled spring, ready to unleash savagery with precise economy of movement. A weapon honed from years of training and blood-soaked necessity.

I glanced over my shoulder, checking the deserted street. This was hardly the place for my full confession. But perhaps, for now, a taste to tease his appetite.

Stepping nearer, I raked my gaze over him slowly. "Let's just say, I'm not all books and tea." I leaned in, relishing the catch of his breath as my lips grazed his ear. "I'm also leather and steel. Smoke and gunpowder."

Drawing back, I searched his face, alert for any reaction. But instead of the shock I expected, his eyes smoldered with something far more dangerous.

Lust.

"I've known enemies too," he said roughly. "Perhaps we're not so different, you and I."

My instincts screamed both warning and desire. Thomas was proving even more unpredictable than anticipated. And God help me, but I wanted him. Wanted that wicked mind and roguish charm between my sheets again, danger be damned.

But there were things we both needed to share first.

I stepped back deliberately. "Come with me," I said coolly. "I think it's time we had a proper talk."

Turning, I led him down the mist-shrouded street toward

the bookshop, hyperaware of his presence at my back. My mind spun with questions. Just how much did Thomas really guess of my past? What secrets of his own did he hide?

And when we finished this dangerous dance of truths, would we wind up friends...or enemies?

Only one way to find out.

Several minutes later, I unlocked the bookshop door and ushered him inside, then upstairs to my private rooms. Once inside, I shrugged off my coat and stoked up the fire, considering how to begin.

Thomas sprawled on my settee, maddeningly at ease. "Shall I guess what you are?" he mused. "A lady sheriff, dispensing justice where the law fails? The secret vigilante scourge, vanquishing London's evildoers?"

Despite myself, I laughed. "Not quite. Do you think I'd look good in a cape and mask?"

His gaze smoldered. "I think you'd look good in anything. Or nothing."

Desire flickered, but I gestured for him to settle. "Patience. We've much to discuss before we...negotiate those kinds of matters."

Sitting across from him, I gathered my thoughts. Some secrets were mine alone to share, yet I'd already decided Thomas could prove a useful partner, hadn't I? Both in chasing the pleasure I'd already had a delicious taste of, and in bringing men like Stanton to justice.

Perhaps a gesture of trust was warranted.

"Very well," I said evenly. "I'll tell you my story, if you swear it goes no further."

He nodded. "Of course."

"I was a spy, Thomas. For the British government. Trained from girlhood in the arts of deception, infiltration, and death. I honed my skills for queen and country, until..."

Until the day I could no longer stomach the work. Until the blood on my hands drowned out the accolades for duty done. Until I walked away from that vicious world, faking my death and making a quiet new life.

But that was too much, too soon. Thomas watched me intently, waiting for me to continue. So I gave him the safer version.

"Until I left that life behind me. I was good at what I did, but it came at a price. Now I use my skills more judiciously, without the constraints of orders or oversight."

Thomas nodded slowly, eyes calculating. "So you turned rogue agent, then. And only serve when the cause warrants it." He smiled slightly. "Am I close?"

"Close enough." There was more truth in his words than I cared to admit. We regarded each other a moment before I raised a brow. "Your turn. How does a handsome scoundrel like yourself occupy his days?"

He laughed, low and soft. "My past is far less colorful than yours, I'm afraid. I'm merely a gentleman of leisure these days."

My snort conveyed my skepticism. Thomas was no random wastrel, I'd stake my life on that.

"Come now," I pressed. "A man like you has stories to tell. I showed you mine..." I let the offer linger.

He paused, then gave a resigned chuckle. "Clever woman. Very well, I was a bit of an adventurer in my youth. Made my fortune in trade overseas before retiring here to enjoy the fruits of my labors."

He wasn't lying, yet I sensed crucial omissions. I fixed him with an expectant look and stayed silent.

Finally, he sighed. "And if certain enterprises occasionally fell outside the strict letter of the law, well, I sleep quite soundly."

Interesting. The picture came into sharper focus. Thomas played a long game too, and wasn't above getting his hands dirty. We were perhaps more alike than I'd assumed.

"I appreciate you being selective with your facts," I said dryly. "But I think we've progressed past pretense, don't you?"

"That we have." He eyed me with new appreciation. "You're wasted keeping dusty books, Elizabeth. With your skills, you could have the world at your feet."

"And what would I do with the world?" I mused. "I've no designs on riches or power. I want only to help those who need it. And to bring men like Stanton to justice."

At the name, Thomas stiffened. "Stanton," he repeated grimly. "Yes, he's long overdue for a reckoning."

I studied him with sudden suspicion. His hatred ran deep; this was no abstract disdain for corruption.

"You have history with him," I guessed.

Thomas's jaw tightened, but he inclined his head. "I do. But that's a tale for another time." His tone warned against pressing for more.

I filed the information away for later. Clearly Stanton had earned Thomas's enmity through personal grievance. Another piece of a most intriguing puzzle.

For now, though, I'd learned enough. Thomas was a scoundrel, but an honorable one. And a man of rare intellect and perception, qualities useful for the fight ahead. Qualities I found most appealing indeed, if I cared to admit it.

Which brought us to the crossroads of this late night.

"If you really want to help, there is a certain gentlemen's club I have an interest in infiltrating," I said. "I believe it to be a den of corrupt aristocrats. Even some association with Lord Stanton."

Thomas's blue eyes glinted with interest. "Go on."

"I intend to infiltrate this place, the Corinthian Club, to find out what I can and uncover more about his associations and activities."

Thomas stroked his chin thoughtfully. "A daring plan, to be sure. You'll need proper resources to pull it off." A roguish grin crossed his face. "Lucky for you, I have access to certain...tools that may be useful."

My pulse quickened. "What did you have in mind?"

"Leave the details to me," Thomas said confidently. "Meet me at Worthington Lane tonight. And we'll give those arrogant bastards a little surprise."

Intrigued by his audaciousness, I agreed to his plan. If

anyone could help me infiltrate the club unnoticed, it was Thomas.

When we met at the rendezvous point, Thomas revealed his preparations. For me, he had acquired a disguise - the uniform of a young servant boy.

"They won't give a lad cleaning the tables a second glance," he explained with a wink.

For himself, he was dressed in an aristocrat's fine coat and hat, looking every inch the wealthy gentleman. No need for disguise there. He had also secured a carriage to convey us to the club inconspicuously. I had to admit, I was impressed by Thomas's ingenuity.

As the carriage clopped through the lamp-lit streets, I adjusted my disguise in the small mirror Thomas provided. With my hair tucked under a cap and oversized clothes hiding my form, I was confident I could pass for a boy.

Soon, the elegant facade of the gentlemen's club emerged from the fog. It was a grand three-story building, glowing with enough lanterns to guide a ship lost at sea. Even from the street, the smell of cigar smoke and brandy permeated the air.

The broad-shouldered doorman scrutinized us briefly before allowing us to enter. Thomas walked with the casual arrogance of a man accustomed to exclusive clubs. I trailed him, keeping my head down.

Inside, the club buzzed with activity – laughter and clinking glasses, and the sound of the rich getting richer. Thomas immediately blended into the surroundings, striking up conversations with nearby gentlemen. His animated storytelling quickly had them chortling and guffawing.

Under the cover of Thomas's distractions, I moved stealthily between the tables, scanning for anything of use. The room was filled with wealthy aristocrats, but none who were obvious associates of Stanton. I maintained my disguise, clearing glasses and wiping down tables.

After twenty minutes of this, I was growing frustrated.

There seemed to be nothing here to aid my mission against Stanto—

And then I spotted him.

At a corner table, half-concealed by shadows, was Lord Henry Blackwood, Stanton's right-hand man. He was scribbling something in a small leather ledger - likely recording illicit business dealings. When finished, he slipped it into his front vest pocket.

My pulse raced at this stroke of luck. Here was a prime opportunity to gain an advantage over Stanton. But stealing the ledger would require perfect timing.

I made my way toward Blackwood's table, maintaining the guise of an efficient servant boy. As I neared him, Thomas launched into a boisterous tale about a hunting escapade, sparking raucous laughter from the nearby gentlemen.

Under cover of his distraction, and the guise of clearing a dish from the table, I deftly slipped the ledger from Blackwood's pocket, concealing it in my oversized sleeve. My heart pounded as I moved away, ledger secured.

I was nearly in the clear when Blackwood suddenly patted his vest pocket, a puzzled frown on his face. I froze. Had he noticed the missing ledger already? If he raised an alarm now, I was doomed – the guards at the door wouldn't let a servant slip out in the middle of a shift without questioning them.

I needed another way out.

I ducked into the next room and grabbed a maid's apron and cap, throwing them on as quickly as I could, tucking the book into the pocket of my new apron. In thirty seconds, I was striding purposefully toward Thomas and without warning, I drew back and slapped him hard across the face.

The crack echoed, the room falling silent.

"You cad! You told me I was the only one!" I shouted in an accusing tone.

Thomas's eyes widened in surprise before he caught on to my ploy. "You ungrateful wench," he bellowed. "How dare you strike me!"

The gentlemen erupted into astonished murmurs and shouts at our dramatic scene. Under cover of the chaos, Thomas and I slipped out of the room for "privacy" and then out of the club before the ruse unraveled.

Safely back in the carriage, Thomas rubbed his cheek ruefully. "Quite a solid performance in there, though you could have pulled your slap a bit. My face will be stinging for a week." Despite his complaint, he grinned at me. "We do make an excellent team though, Miss Templeton."

I gave a reluctant chuckle. "It seems we do, Mr. Callahan." I patted my pocket where the precious ledger waited. "And it appears this partnership has borne valuable fruit tonight."

Thomas inclined his head in agreement. "I believe unraveling the secrets in that ledger may just be the key to undermining Stanton's whole wretched operation."

I hoped he was right.

An hour later, I finally had a chance to examine our hard-won prize. The stolen ledger lay open on my desk in the candlelight as Thomas and I pored over the cramped lines filling its pages.

"Look here," Thomas said, pointing to a column of numbers. "Blackwood records payments of hundreds of pounds every month to someone labeled only as 'Magistrate A'. Do you think he's bribing the authorities?"

I nodded grimly, my anger rising as I scanned the ledger. "That's undoubtedly the case. And there seem to be similar payments made to 'Lord B', 'Officer C', and so on. Stanton has this entire city in his pocket through bribes and blackmail."

Thomas's expression matched my own disgust. "The scale of his corruption is staggering. He wields power like a criminal puppet master."

My eyes darted rapidly across the ledger as the scope of Stanton's empire unfolded before me. Magistrates, lords, inspectors, officers - all under his control through illicit payments and threats. It was a web of corruption beyond anything I had imagined.

For a long moment, I was silent, considering the implications. Then I looked up and met Thomas's gaze.

"This changes everything. With this evidence, we can rip apart Stanton's entire rotten empire. Everyone he manipulates into doing his dirty work - we can free them from his control."

Thomas nodded firmly, a fierce light in his blue eyes. "Then let this be the first strike that brings his corrupt reign crashing down."

I nodded, tapping my finger on the ledger. "We need to be where these people—the upper crust of London—are."

Thomas's mouth twitched into a smirk. "I think I know just the place."

Chapter 9

The sun may have set on London hours ago, but the city was alive with light. I stood at my bedroom window, peering out at the growing parade of England's party-goers making grand entrances. In a few moments I would join them, decked in green silk that hugged my curves tighter than a Scotsman clings to his whisky. Tonight, I would enter enemy territory.

I turned from the window with a swish of emerald skirts. I had sewn discreet inner pockets into the gown to hold my lock picking tools and other necessary trinkets. A curved dagger was sheathed at my thigh, easily accessible through a slit in the dress yet invisible to prying eyes. I slid the blade into place and ensured it wouldn't slip free. Satisfied with my preparations, I moved to the vanity and arranged my hair into an elegant updo, leaving a few curled tendrils to frame my face.

The final piece of my disguise sat on the vanity: an ornate green and gold masquerade mask adorned with peacock feathers that fanned out to the sides. I lifted the mask to my face, feathers caressing my cheeks.

As I tied it in place, I caught my reflection in the mirror. My ensemble was complete, my real purpose cloaked in elegance. To any other guest, I was every inch the mysterious minx, but little did anyone know that I was on a mission.

A knock sounded at the bedroom door and I opened it to find Thomas on the other side, looking so sharp in his suit I could slice myself on him, his half mask unable to disguise the admiration in his eyes, looking at me like I was the last shot of bourbon at closing time.

"Good lord, Elizabeth," he breathed. "You look..." Words

seemed to fail him as he took in the sight of me. Under different circumstances, I might have reveled in rendering him speechless. But such fancies would have to wait for a time when the fate of London itself wasn't at stake.

"Ready, I hope?" I said briskly. When Thomas simply continued to stare, eyes roaming in a most inappropriate fashion, I gave an impatient huff. "Chop-chop, evil waits for no woman."

Thomas blinked, shaking himself out of his daze. "Yes, yes of course," he said, offering his arm. "Shall we?"

I took his arm and we descended the stairs, the swish of my skirts and click of my heels the only sounds in the hushed bookshop. At the door, Thomas handed me into an ornate carriage befitting the night's charade. As we rolled down the darkened London streets, I steeled myself for the task ahead.

The Mayfair mansion loomed before us, blazing with light, music and chatter already spilling from its windows. As Thomas helped me out, I peered at the place, feeling my blood sizzle. To think that behind these fine walls, vile schemes might be hatching. Even now some of these men probably toasted their ill-gotten gains, thinking they were untouchable.

We strutted up the steps arm in arm. At the entrance, a liveried footman checked our invitation and ushered us inside. We were swept into a glittering sea of silks and masks, the light from the chandeliers splintering into prismatic splendor. An orchestra played a lively waltz to which elegantly dressed couples danced and spun. Though outwardly I smiled, inwardly I cataloged each hallway and staircase, mapping routes of access and escape. Thomas led me forward, nodding politely to the various lords and ladies who filled the ballroom, likely unaware they cavorted with snakes.

"I don't suppose you'd care to dance?" Thomas asked, raising an eyebrow with a suggestive smirk, as if he wasn't proposing a twirl on the dance floor but something far more scandalous in the broom closet.

I eyed the gyrating mass of aristocrats. A dance might grant us greater access to the less visible reaches of the ballroom. On the other hand, maintaining vigilance would prove difficult in all that constant motion.

"I think not," I decided, tugging him toward the balcony, "Let's go pretend to be star-crossed lovers in need of fresh air instead."

Out on the terrace, the night was painting its best seduction scene, all soft breezes and Chinese lanterns swinging as if they were trying to hypnotize us. Couples and small groups clustered here and there, speaking in hushed tones or staring dreamily out at the night sky. Thomas and I situated ourselves unobtrusively near a leafy alcove, the music and chatter from within fading to a distant murmur.

Thomas, ever the plotter, whispered, "Fancy a scandalous stroll through the shrubbery? Might find a back door or a loose window we can utilize later."

I nodded agreement and took his proffered arm. We descended the terrace steps and strolled casually along the graveled paths that wound through the sculpted hedges and flower beds of the estate gardens. To any observer we appeared an ordinary pair slipping away for a tryst amidst the roses. Only we knew our true purpose as we scouted every gate, alcove and garden shed.

Satisfied with our surveillance, we looped back toward the mansion. As we reached the terrace, raucous laughter drew our eyes up. There, on a first-floor balcony, stood a paunchy, red-faced man gesturing wildly as he regaled his companions with some tale or other. I tensed. The weasel in a waistcoat himself, Lord Marcus Stanton.

Thomas's arm tightened beneath my hand. "Easy," he cautioned. "We need to bide our time." I forced my muscles to relax, though my fury simmered beneath the surface. The gall of the man, living it up while innocents like Amelia cowered in the darkness.

Schooling my features into pleasant indifference, I allowed Thomas to lead me back inside. We drifted from room to room, blending seamlessly into the sea of masked revelers while covertly taking note of side doors and shadowed hallways. I surveyed the crowd, picking out faces I recognized from the intelligence Thomas and I had gathered. These were Stanton's associates in corruption, the facilitators of his many misdeeds. How blissfully ignorant they seemed, laughing and drinking without a care. Let them enjoy this last shining moment before their world collapsed around them.

My eyes inevitably drifted back to Stanton's balcony. He had moved inside but I could just glimpse his silver head, no doubt spinning grand designs and congratulating himself on his untouchable position. The dagger strapped to my leg was practically vibrating with the urge to leap out and introduce itself to his black heart.

Soon, you bastard, I thought.

"Easy," Thomas murmured, following my gaze. "And wisdom. We're playing chess, not checkers. Keep your queen hidden until it's time to strike."

I nodded tightly. He was right, of course. I couldn't let my thirst for justice mess up our carefully laid plans.

Though, I couldn't help but think one quick tango with destiny wouldn't hurt.

"I suppose one dance couldn't hurt," I said, as I let him lead me onto the floor, joining the swirl of color and light.

We waltzed into the fray, but while Thomas was light on his feet, my mind was heavy with schemes. Every step, every turn, every beat of the music was background noise to the gears turning in my head. I was here for one purpose only - to find proof of Stanton's corruption and connections to the disappearances that had been plaguing the city.

My eyes flickered around the ballroom, cataloguing possible threats.

The dance ended and Thomas and I drifted apart like two ships passing in the night, mingling amongst the other guests, pretending to give a shit about their boring conversations. I snagged another glass of champagne from a passing waiter and scanned the room, looking for a potential rat. Who here might be willing to stab their lord and master in the back? My eyes landed on a rotund gentleman with a face as red as a baboon's ass, which spoke of a fondness for port. Perhaps loosening his lips could loosen his secrets as well.

With a dazzling smile, I strutted over, ready to turn on the charm. We spoke lightly of the weather and other trivialities. But when I casually steered the conversation toward Stanton, a shadow crossed his face. He muttered some lame excuse and hightailed it out of there. One by one, my subtle attempts to extract information from various partygoers were met with fear or loyalty. These guys had been handpicked, carefully selected from Stanton's flock of ass-kissing sycophants. I wasn't going to find any willing snitches here.

A cold prickle on the back of my neck alerted me that someone was watching my every move. I turned slowly, casting my gaze across the room. And that's when I saw her. A tall, imposing figure dressed in a silver gown, an elegant fox mask perched on her harsh features. Recognition slammed through me and I had to suppress a startled gasp. Her eyes met mine through the crowd, two chips of pale blue ice. Even from across the room, I could feel the weight of that piercing gaze.

Lady Victoria Caldwell.

I never expected to see that woman again, not since we had crossed paths all those years ago. She had a reputation that could scare the devil himself—ruthless, cunning, and completely devoid of any moral compass. She'd been one of the Agency's most effective operatives until she disappeared under suspicious circumstances. Most assumed she had turned traitor and been quietly eliminated. Yet here she stood, very much alive.

Caldwell eased through the crowd toward me, an elegant fox on the hunt. I straightened my spine and prepared to face her. We exchanged cool pleasantries, but underneath the surface, it was a silent battle of wills.

"Elizabeth, darling," she said, her voice dripping with venom. "What an unexpected surprise. "Keeping out of trouble, I trust?"

Her words carried an undercurrent of threat. She knew exactly what I'd been up to. I gave a nonchalant laugh. "Just enjoying a simple life out of the spotlight. Although I must say, events seem to have taken quite an interesting turn lately." I held her icy gaze steadily. "Though I'm sure you know more about that than I do."

Her smirk was as sharp as a guillotine blade. "Indeed. Lord Stanton has been most accommodating opening his home to me. We shall have to...catch up further very soon."

I nodded, acknowledging the unspoken message between us. Caldwell was working with Stanton, but I had no clue what their endgame was. One thing was certain though - she had her own ruthless agenda. This painted everything in a far grimmer light. I wasn't just dealing with some power-hungry lord anymore; I was up against a dangerous mind, the kind I hadn't encountered since my days in the Agency.

I finished our conversation with subtle warnings of my own, promising an imminent reckoning. We parted ways cordially, two predators temporarily retreating to our respective corners. I needed to tread carefully. Caldwell was not to be underestimated.

The ball swirled around me as I retreated to the fringes of the room, moving silently through the shadows. Thomas materialized at my side, ever attuned to the darkness.

"Who was that?" he asked, his voice hushed and heavy.

I briefly filled him in on Caldwell's history and my suspicions. He nodded grimly.

"We need to get out of here, quickly and quietly," I told him. "My presence here will have raised too many questions now that Caldwell is involved."

He inclined his head and went to fetch our carriage as I slipped into the crowd making their way to the entrance. The night air was crisp and cool against my flushed skin.

Thomas pulled the carriage up moments later, and we made our escape from the glittering palace of secrets. I didn't look back as we rode away, the mansion fading into the distance, but I could still feel Caldwell's icy gaze burning into me, and a chill settled deep in my bones. Shit had just gotten a whole lot more complicated and dangerous.

My mind continued dissecting each piece as we drove home, but it was like grasping at smoke - no matter how I tried to connect the threads, the full picture eluded me. Caldwell's presence changed the game entirely. I needed more information.

We soon arrived back at my quiet home. I bade Thomas a good night at the door; we agreed it was best for him not to stick around tonight – we couldn't afford the distraction.

I turned the key in the lock and stepped into the familiar warmth of my sanctuary, shed of finery and pretense. But as I lit a lamp in the cozy sitting room, my eyes fell on something that froze my blood - a letter on the sideboard, written in an unfamiliar hand. My fingers trembled as I broke the seal and read the short, bone-chilling message.

We have Amelia.

Chapter 10

At some point, I'd fallen into a fitful sleep filled with images of Amelia, hurt and helpless. I paced my bookshop the next morning, fuming over the lack of usable evidence I had against Stanton. All I could think about was bringing that bastard down, making him pay for everything he'd done. But without concrete proof, my hands were tied. I needed a new plan, and I needed it fast.

My furious pacing was interrupted by the bells above the door as Jacob poked his head in. My mood instantly lifted at the sight of the boy's messy sandy hair and bright eyes. He was here for his usual delivery run.

"Morning, Miss Elizabeth," Jacob said, giving me a grin that showed every bit of his mischievous nature. The kid was barely twelve but he could always make me smile.

His arrival sparked an idea. I knew Jacob spent a lot of time lurking around the streets and alleys near the bank. If anyone could get intel on Stanton, maybe it was him.

Before I could second guess myself, I made the offer.

"Jacob, I have a special job for you if you're interested. I'll pay you well—enough to feed yourself for months."

The boy's eyes went wide. "What kind of job?" he asked.

"I need information on a man named Stanton who frequents the bank. Anything you can find out about his dealings there would be useful."

Jacob looked uncertain. I didn't blame him. What I was asking was dangerous. But we both knew he could use the money, and it was a good excuse for me to help him in that department – he was always too proud to accept charity.

After a long moment, he nodded. "Alright Miss Elizabeth, you've got yourself a deal."

I let out a breath. This was a risk, getting Jacob involved, but I was desperate. I gave him half the payment upfront and sent him on his way.

Over the next two days, I waited anxiously for Jacob to return with news. But he didn't come. By the third day, I was a mess of nerves. I had no way to contact him—if anything happened to that boy...

I couldn't sit around any longer. There was only one person I could ask for help.

One look at my worried expression and Thomas was on high alert. "What's happened?" he asked.

I quickly explained the situation. "We need to check the slums, see if anyone has seen Jacob."

Thomas nodded, his face grim. He knew as well as I did that finding one street kid in the maze of filthy alleys and ramshackle buildings wasn't going to be easy. But we had to try.

We spent hours combing the streets, asking anyone we encountered about Jacob. Most just glared at us, spitting on the ground near our polished boots—the presence of a lady and a fancy gentleman clearly wasn't welcome. But we persisted.

Finally, as we were about to give up hope, a scrawny girl pointed towards a narrow alley. "Check there," she muttered before scurrying into the shadows.

Thomas and I hurried to the dim, cramped passage.

Jacob sat slumped against the wall, his small body a patchwork of bruises and dirt. I barely recognized him.

"Oh my god," I gasped, rushing over. Jacob gave me a pained smile.

"I got it Miss Elizabeth," he said hoarsely, holding up a bundle of papers. Bank records, from the looks of it. I wanted to sob—what had I done? But there was no time for that. I needed to get Jacob help.

Thomas scooped the boy into his arms. I tossed a few coins

to the wide-eyed girl who'd helped us as I followed.

We brought Jacob to a discreet clinic I knew of from my time in the field. The doctor was surprised but didn't ask questions when I handed him a hefty payment to care for the boy.

"Give him anything he needs," I ordered. "Spare no expense."

The doctor nodded and carried Jacob to the back room.

Finally, I allowed myself to break down. Thomas wrapped me in his strong arms as I cried. This was all my fault. I never should have gotten Jacob involved.

"You were trying to do the right thing," Thomas said gently. "We'll make sure he's okay."

Over the next few days, I practically lived at the clinic. I sat by Jacob's bedside as he drifted in and out of feverish sleep. I brought him books and sweets, reading to him when he was awake. My heart broke seeing his small body wracked with pain.

But slowly, he started to recover.

When Jacob was finally strong enough, I showed him the bank records he'd risked his life to get. My instincts were right—the documents revealed a web of suspicious transactions all linked to Stanton. If I could trace the money trail, I might be able to expose that bastard's crimes.

I tried to thank Jacob, but the words died in my throat. The boy was looking at me with such steadfast loyalty despite everything he'd endured. In that moment, something shifted inside me. Jacob was no longer just an errand boy. He was my responsibility, and I would do anything to keep him from harm.

"Miss Elizabeth?" Jacob said hesitantly. "Are you alright?"

I quickly wiped a stray tear from my cheek. "Yes. Thanks to you." I squeezed his hand, my voice thick with emotion.

Jacob gave me a grin. "So does this mean I get a bonus?"

I laughed—a real, full belly laugh—and pulled him into a fierce hug. We stayed like that for a long moment, the tragedy of the past few days fading into a flicker of hope for the future.

As I made my way home from the clinic, my mind churned over recent events. Jacob had proven himself brave and loyal beyond his years. He'd risked everything to help me, and nearly paid the ultimate price. I was overwhelmed with guilt for putting him in harm's way, but also filled with admiration for his selfless courage.

I dove headfirst into analyzing the bank records Jacob had managed to snag, tracing Stanton's shady transactions. The web was complex, but I steadily untangled it, exhilarated by each new revelation. Stanton had his grubby hands in all sorts of shady dealings—money laundering, blackmail, extortion. If I could find enough evidence, I could bring down his whole corrupt empire. For the first time, it was starting to feel like that was possible.

A note arrived on a blustery Tuesday afternoon, delivered by a raggedy kid I'd never seen before. He shoved it into my hand, his eyes darting like a scared rabbit, before scampering back into the bustling London streets. The wax seal caught my eye immediately - an elaborate emblem of a rearing horse that I knew belonged to Lady Caldwell.

My pulse quickened as I broke the seal and unfolded the letter. The message was short and ominous:

Meet me at Windermere Manor tonight at eight. Come alone. Caldwell.

I read it three times, a knot forming in my stomach. Caldwell was not a woman to be trifled with. Crossing her was unwise at best and fatal at worst.

But she could have information I needed. She could have Amelia.

I burned the note in the fireplace, watching the flames consume the elegant stationary.

Windermere Manor waited on the outskirts of London like a hulking beast from another time. Once a grand estate, it had fallen into decay since the last owner kicked the bucket. Ivy crawled up its crumbling walls and weeds choked what remained of the gardens.

It was also the place where I had trained my ass off, alongside Caldwell. The elite of the elite in the spy business had all spent time there, sharpening our skills and intellect.

As I approached, the setting sun cast an orange glow on the manor's highest peaks. But at ground level, a damp chill already hung in the air. I pulled my cloak tighter, as much against the cold as the sense of unease swirling in my gut.

This was a dangerous game. But the siren song of truth drew me forward.

At exactly eight o'clock, I rapped the lion head door knocker against the warped oak door. The sound echoed ominously across the grounds. For several long moments, only silence answered.

Just as I raised my hand to knock again, the door creaked open. A hulking man with a face made of scars gestured for me to enter. Swallowing my nerves, I stepped into the gloom of Windermere Manor.

The interior matched the decaying exterior, all moth-eaten curtains and peeling wallpaper. Our footsteps echoed across the bare floors as the man led me down a musty hallway. Cobwebs draped the faded portraits adorning the walls, almost as if the house was somehow haunted by its former grandeur.

At the end of the hall the elegant woman stood, silhouetted in candlelight. Though well into her fifties, her silver hair was styled impeccably, not a strand out of place. Her ice blue eyes watched me approach with a hawk's intensity.

"Lady Caldwell." I kept my tone light, belying the tension coiling through my body.

"Elizabeth Templeton." She inclined her head in greeting. "I'm pleased you accepted my invitation. Please, sit."

I settled into the proffered chair, hyper aware of the two armed men flanking Caldwell like statues. She sat with perfect posture, emanating the very image of aristocratic poise. But there was a ruthless glint in her eyes that betrayed the facade.

"I must admit, I was quite intrigued by your note," I began, crossing one leg casually over the other. "I can't imagine what urgent business you and I could have together."

A chilling smile curved her lips. "I have a proposition for you, Miss Templeton. One I think you'll find most…enticing."

My eyes narrowed, but before I could respond, she snapped her fingers. The scarred man who had led me inside approached, holding a polished wooden box. He placed it reverently on the table between us.

Caldwell ran one manicured nail across the box, then flipped the latch and lifted the lid. Inside, on a bed of velvet, lay a gold pocket watch.

My heart seized at the sight. I knew that watch. Knew every groove and scratch in its burnished surface. It had belonged to James Hayden, a close colleague, and occasionally more…who had been killed in a fluke accident eight years ago.

"Surprised?" Caldwell's smile turned predatory. "I thought you might recognize this."

"That's impossible." I choked out. "That watch was buried with…"

"With James? Such a shame, cut down in his prime the way he was." Her voice dripped false sympathy. "Terrible tragedy, that. Although…" She leaned forward, her words dropping to a conspiratorial whisper. "Perhaps not quite the random incident it appeared."

Hot rage flooded my veins, momentarily overtaking my shock. This vile woman knew James had been murdered. Had known all along, and let everyone believe it was an accident.

I surged to my feet, hands curling into fists. The guards tensed, but Caldwell lifted a hand, her eyes glinting with amusement.

"Did you order his death?" I demanded through gritted teeth. Caldwell's smile only widened at the accusation.

"Come now, Miss Templeton," she chided. "Let's not resort to unpleasantries. I simply wanted to…clarify some facts. James's death was necessary for the circumstances at hand. Collateral damage. You understand."

Collateral damage. As if James's life had meant nothing. As if my world hadn't shattered when he'd been ripped away.

"You cold-blooded bitch." My voice shook with fury. "I'll see you rot for this."

Caldwell glanced at the pocket watch lazily. "Well, as entertaining as this has been, I'm on a schedule, so I'll get right to the point - I want you to join my organization, Miss Templeton."

"Like hell," I spat.

"You didn't let me finish," she admonished. "I'm offering you power beyond anything you could imagine. Together we could rule London's underworld, puppet masters pulling the strings of its pathetic police force and corrupt politicians."

She rose and began circling me like a shark, her words flowing smooth as honey. "I've been watching you and I see a kindred spirit. A ruthless ambition, an appetite for control, a distaste for the trivial rules that bind ordinary men. You have talents I can refine, a mind I can sculpt into something glorious. Deny it all you like, but I know your true potential."

I stood motionless as she prowled, refusing to be intimidated. When she finished her circuit, she leaned in close, her breath hot on my ear.

"Join me, Elizabeth. Seize the power you deserve. Say yes, and you need never bow to anyone again. We could be unstoppable."

I met her gaze unflinchingly. "The only thing I'll help you seize is the inside of a jail cell. I don't know what depraved fantasy you've concocted about me, but the only potential I plan on realizing is bringing you to an end."

Caldwell's eyes hardened to ice. For a long moment, we stared each other down in silence. Then she stepped back, a cool smile on her lips once more.

"A pity." She raised a hand languidly. "If you won't join me, I'm afraid I can't have you interfering with my operations." She turned to one of her goons. "Kill her."

The guards sprang into action before her words had fully left her lips. I dove to the side as a meaty fist swung through the space my head had just occupied. Spinning low, I swept my leg out and sent the man crashing to the ground.

The second guard came at me with a roar, and I slipped into the flow of combat, my training taking over. I struck strategic points - throat, solar plexus, knees - until he stumbled back, wheezing. Behind me, the scarred man had regained his feet and both men rushed me at once.

I leapt onto the table, temporarily gaining higher ground. As they grabbed for my legs, I smashed a vase over one man's head. He went down hard. The other I dispatched with a solid kick to the temple that made a sickening crack.

Chest heaving, I turned to find Caldwell gone. The damn snake had slipped away while her men kept me busy. Coward.

Another time, then. For now, I needed to get out while I still could.

I rushed into the hall, only to hear shouts and pounding footsteps coming from the foyer. More of Caldwell's men, no doubt. I veered left instead, hoping to find a side door.

The hall led past a darkened parlor. I was almost past when a shadow detached from the wall and barreled straight into me. We crashed to the floor in a tangle of limbs, my head hitting with a sickening crack against the hardwood.

Dazed, and being dragged across the dingy carpet, I twisted sharply, breaking the man's grip. Before he could react, I drove my elbow up into his nose. A satisfying crunch echoed through the hall as blood poured from his face.

"You bitch!" another man shouted. He backhanded me hard across the cheek. My head spun, but I used the momentum to wrench free of his hold. I may have been outnumbered, but I still had a few tricks up my sleeve.

My skills in various fighting forms gave me an edge over their brute force, but I was tiring, my movements slowing. A massive fist collided with my ribs and I felt at least fractured, white hot pain lancing through my side.

I needed to end this, fast. Spotting a lit candelabra on a side table, I feinted left then grabbed the burning fixture, swinging it in a wide arc. The men fell back with cries of pain as hot wax splattered their faces. Not wasting the opportunity, I sprinted for the nearest doorway.

My breath came in ragged gasps, my side screaming with each stride. I risked a glance back, the men still in pursuit. I couldn't keep this up much longer.

Suddenly, my foot caught on an uneven plank in the floor and I sprawled forward, barely getting my hands out to break my fall. The impact jarred my fractured ribs and I couldn't hold back a scream. For a moment, I lay stunned on the cold ground. Rough hands grabbed at me, dragging me upright.

I lashed out in desperation, my fist connecting with another nose in a spray of blood. A knife glinted in the candlelight and I twisted to avoid the blade, feeling it slice through the fabric of my dress and graze my side. Warm blood soaked through the ripped material.

Ignoring the pain, I smashed my forehead into the man's face, hearing another satisfying crunch of cartilage and bone. He howled, dropping the knife to clutch at his ruined nose. I scooped up the fallen blade, brandishing it wildly. The sight gave the others pause, granting me a few precious seconds to create some distance.

My mind raced, trying to remember the hidden passages riddling the manor. There was one concealed entrance just ahead. I dashed right, stumbling down a darkened stairwell hidden. I eased the hidden door shut and collapsed against it, my breath coming in ragged gasps.

The passage was musty and close, with only a few weak beams of light filtering through cracks in the stone. But it was an escape. I glanced down, gingerly peeling the torn fabric of my dress away from the knife wound in my side. It was bleeding steadily, the warm sticky blood coating my hand when I probed the gash. I ripped a strip of fabric from my petticoat and tied it tightly around my waist, staunching the worst of the flow. It would have to do for now.

I took a few careful steps along the passage, one hand

trailing the rough stone wall for balance. Each movement jarred the bruised, probably broken ribs in my side, the pain nearly blinding. But I forced myself onward, each step taking me farther away.

I nearly wept with relief when I reached the end of the tunnel, pushing open the hidden entrance built into the trees at the edge of the grounds.

My breath rasped loudly in the night air as I stumbled away. My dress was filthy and torn, drenched in blood and sweat. I probably looked half crazed, my hair wild and matted with dirt and cobwebs. But I didn't care. All that mattered was getting as far from that place as possible.

I made it maybe a quarter mile before my legs started to shake, my head spinning with blood loss. I sank to my knees, clawing at the dirt as I tried to push myself back up. It was no use. The world tilted dangerously and I slumped onto my side, darkness creeping into my vision.

No. I couldn't pass out here, so exposed. With my last ounce of strength, I dragged myself into a ditch running along the road, concealing myself beneath a tangle of brambles. My pulse pounded in my ears, my breath coming in short, pained gasps.

Then the darkness took me, my battered body finally giving out.

Chapter 11

I awoke slowly, my mind foggier than a London alley on a misty morning. For a long moment I lay there, face mashed into the dirt, my mind doing a drunken dance trying to remember where the hell I was. The stench of blood and sweat clinging to my skin - it all came rushing back. Windermere Manor. The fight.

The great fucking escape.

With a groan that'd make a warthog proud, I hauled myself upright, every inch of my body protesting. I must have been out cold for a few hours—dawn was just breaking, casting a pale gray light over the surrounding woods. I needed to get my ass out of there, find some cover, and lick my wounds.

My ribs screamed in protest as I staggered to my feet, one arm clutching my side. I clung to a tree like a lovesick leech, sucking in thin breaths between the pulses of pain. Bandages and a hefty swig of brandy were top of my to-do list, but I'd lost my bearings in the chaos of the night.

I scanned the surrounding woods, getting my first good look at the area. A small flicker of hope rose in my chest. If my battered brain wasn't playing tricks, Thomas's estate was a stumble and a stagger away.

I set off through the woods, huffing and puffing like a walrus in a corset with each step. The wound in my side burned like a motherfucker, fresh blood soaking through the makeshift bandage. My legs trembled with the effort to remain upright. But I kept on, following the trails etched into my memory until the imposing walls of Thomas's manor loomed ahead.

I made it as far as the front steps before my legs buckled,

sending me sprawling onto the polished wood like a drunk after last call. Fresh blood flowed from my hands, mingling with the dirt and crusted blood already caking my hands. I crawled my sorry ass up the remaining steps, smearing crimson handprints on the pristine surface. Then I slumped against the carved double doors, darkness creeping at the edge of my vision.

Summoning the last ounce of strength I had left, I pounded my fist against the door once, the heavy thud reverberating through my battered body as I promptly passed out.

I came to with a pained gasp, my whole body taut with agony. Gentle hands grasped my shoulders, easing me back against soft pillows.

"Easy. You're safe now." Thomas's voice rolled over me like a soothing wave, calming the panic that came with waking up feeling like I'd gone straight through the wringer.

I pried my eyes open, squinting against the brightness. Heavy velvet curtains blocked most of the morning sun, leaving the room in muted light. I was in Thomas's bed, propped up on a pile of pillows. Clean white bandages wrapped my ribs, a small spot of red bleeding through over the knife wound. Freshly salved cuts and bruises covered my hands and arms.

I winced as I gingerly touched the tender spot near my temple, feeling the swollen bump beneath my fingertips. Definitely going to be a nasty bruise there. I took stock of the rest of my injuries - some deep muscle aches along my ribs, and the fierce stinging of the gash along my side. Caldwell's thugs had done a number on me, but at least I'd given as good as I got.

"What the hell happened?" Thomas asked from the seat beside me. His voice was quiet but taut.

I blew out a long breath, gathering the whirlwind of thoughts spinning through my pounding head. "I met with Caldwell. Had a lovely little chat that ended with her goons trying to use me as a punching bag." Thomas's jaw clenched at my flippant tone, but he remained silent.

"Obviously things got...heated. But I gave them the slip and eventually high-tailed it out of there. Maybe took a tumble here and there in the process. You know how clumsy I can be," I added with a weak smile.

Thomas didn't crack a grin. His stony expression and terse silence prompted me to continue.

"I'm okay, really. Just feel like I got trampled by a horse. A small herd of horses." I tried for levity again, but Thomas was clearly not in the mood.

I sighed, my mirth fading. "It was actually rather informative, all things considered. Caldwell was spouting all sorts of nonsense about me targeting her, wanting to ruin her life. She's paranoid as all hell."

Thomas's brow furrowed. "That's madness. Why would she think you'd have some personal vendetta against her?"

I shook my head slowly. "That's just it - it's not personal for me. But for her, it is. Everything comes back to control. She feels the need to control every aspect of her life. I think she hoped meeting with me directly would intimidate me into backing down, and bring me under her control. Doesn't excuse the violence, of course. She's clearly unstable, and desperate to hold onto her power."

My ribs protested as I took a deep breath and continued. "She tried to recruit me over to her side, right after she revealed she killed one of our colleagues years ago."

Thomas glanced up, his eyes glinting knowingly. "I'm sorry," he said, his tone somber. "She must realize her house of cards is on shaky ground. You snooping around has her and Stanton freaking out."

I nodded. "She knows Stanton's operation has vulnerabilities, and she's terrified of losing...whatever it is she thinks she has. This," I said, generally motioning at my battered body, "was about intimidation and re-establishing control, even if it's only in her own mind."

He studied my face intently. "So you shook Caldwell's confidence. But it also put you directly in harm's way. Again." His jaw tightened, something dark brewing behind his eyes.

"At least now we have a clearer picture of her motivations. She's desperate to grow her power and status. And that makes her vulnerable." I straightened up with a wince, determination burning through the lingering pain and fatigue. "Which means now is the time to keep pressing our advantage. She's unstable, making mistakes. We need to keep exploiting the cracks in Stanton's network."

Adrenaline surged in me, honing my focus.

Thomas tensed. But I couldn't decipher the storm brewing in those eyes, the muscles feathering along his clenched jaw, the line between his brows that signaled barely restrained emotion.

This silence was somehow more unnerving than any outburst.

Finally, he spoke. "This has to stop, Elizabeth. I thought I was ready for this, for whatever came our way, but seeing you like this…." He shook his head roughly. "No more of these reckless plans. No more putting yourself in harm's way." His voice was low but razor sharp.

I recoiled as his words sliced through me.

And of course, my temper flared in response. "This is my choice to make, Thomas. My fight. You don't get to decide what risks I take." I held his blazing stare unflinchingly.

He surged to his feet, turning away with a harsh laugh. "Your choice? It stopped being just your choice when your actions started affecting the people around you." He spun back around, hands clenched. "What about Jacob? And then finding you here, bloodied and beaten half to death? When does it end, Elizabeth?"

The quiet devastation in his words pierced my simmering anger. I took a shaky breath, trying to calm the clashing emotions within me. "Thomas, you know I'm not doing this for selfish reasons. This is about justice, about protecting people like Amelia from monsters like Stanton."

I leaned toward him. "I can't stand by when I have the power to stop such evil. Not when I know what they're capable of. What they've already done." My voice cracked over the last words.

Thomas's rigid posture softened marginally at my vulnerable admission. He reached out and gently tucked a loose curl behind my ear, skimming his fingers along my cheek. "I know your intentions are good, Elizabeth. That you want to help people. But..."

He dropped his hand with a pained sigh. "I can't keep watching you fighting these battles. Not when the cost is so high. If it were just about me, I could maybe accept choosing danger for the sake of conviction. But watching you—and Jacob—pay the price...I just can't." His eyes were bleak, haunted. "It has to stop."

My temper surged again, a shield against the dread. "So you expect me to just stand back and do nothing? What? Because I'm a woman? But danger is okay for you? Even though I started this, I'm just supposed to let Stanton keep destroying lives while I, someone with the skills and information to actually stop him go quietly back to my books as if I'm not still haunted by it all?" I balled my hands into fists. "I won't ignore my conscience and give up the chance for justice just because you ask it of me."

Thomas gazed at me with infinite sadness. "No. I suppose you won't. You're too damned brave for your own good." His voice was weary, stripped of anger.

He reached out and traced his finger along the bruise on my temple.

"I know we said we'd work together, but this...it's too much." He squared his shoulders as if steadying his resolve. "I refuse to play a part in it anymore." His eyes glistened. "I can't watch you kill yourself."

With that he stood, his retreating steps echoing with a deafening finality across the expansive room.

Chapter 12

The stillness was broken only by the scratch of my quill against parchment as I scribbled every detail I uncovered—mostly through Blackwood's journal—about Cassius, Stanton's quiet and unassuming accountant. But the unassuming part was just an act. The information I compiled filled page after page – with a special focus on two things, his visits to the local massage parlour known for providing special services, and invoices for shipments of rare and expensive wines delivered to his home. In the margins I'd scribbled second-hand accounts I had carefully coaxed from chatty barmaids who had encountered the man.

Cassius struck me as the weakest link in Stanton's operation. While the other men radiated gravitas and commanded fear, Cassius faded into the background, more occupied with ledgers and figures than with the shady dealings that kept Stanton's coffers filled. He was a man ruled by his baser desires, flashes of greed and lust breaking through his mild-mannered façade, and I was about to become his favorite sin.

The man was a walking, talking seven deadly sins wrapped in one pudgy, lustful package with a taste for exotic wines, and a weekly visit to Madame Velvetine's for a standard massage followed by one of the special "deluxe" treatments.

His greatest vice was his desire for the unattainable. Which is exactly what I was about to dangle in front of him.

A day later, I stood before the mirror surveying my transformation - the rich velvet gown accentuating my figure, and eyes smoky enough to start a forest fire. I hardly recognized the woman staring back - she was a stranger, an enchantress. My fingers went to my side, pressing lightly to feel the ridge of bandage through the corset I wore over the slice in my side. One last reminder of why I had to succeed today.

With a final deep breath, I stepped outside into the bustling city. The sun was dipping low, casting an amber glow onto the rain slicked streets. Evening was the domain of those who preferred anonymity - of secret trysts and furtive deals. Drawing my cloak tightly around me, I slipped into the swelling crowds making their way toward more lascivious pursuits. None would mark my passing - I was just another shadow seeking distraction as night approached.

Madame Velvetine's was tucked down a dim side alley, discreetly marked with a weathered sign depicting a lotus in bloom. I wrinkled my nose as I stepped inside. The air was cloying, reeking of cheap perfume and desperation mixed with the tartness of wine and the faint hint of sexual odors. My eyes adjusted to the low light, taking in the heavy drapes sectioning off private rooms for entertaining clientele. A piano played languidly in a back corner.

I spotted a woman who could only be Madame Velvetine holding court by a carved mahogany bar. Her dark hair was upswept, lips painted a deep red that matched her gown. She arched a brow that was penciled on so sharp it could cut glass.

"I don't believe we've had the pleasure." Her tone was smooth but her look appraising as she took in my appearance.

"My name is of no importance," I replied evenly. " I'm here for Cassius. He needs some...extra attention tonight." I slipped her a two-pound note.

Understanding lit her widened eyes and she and she smirked like we were old friends sharing a dirty secret. "I see. Well, it's about time Cassius was treated to some new company. I grow so tired of his tediousness." She inclined her head toward a doorway covered by a thick curtain. "He's already here, third room on the left. Do try to get him to open that purse of his a bit wider tonight, won't you dear?"

I forced a coy smile. "Of course, Madame. I intend to provide an experience he won't soon forget."

With a satisfied nod, she dismissed me and turned her attention to a pair of gentlemen seated nearby. "Looks like I'm free after all," she said as I walked away, steeling myself as I moved with measured steps to the curtained doorway, each footfall carrying me closer to what felt like a viper's nest. But I could not afford to waver now. Too much was at stake.

Pushing aside the heavy drapes revealed a dim hallway lined with doors. Muffled sounds emanated from some of the rooms - laughter, cries of passion, groans. I kept my eyes fixed ahead as I navigated past clutching, grunting patrons toward the third curtain on the left. This was not my first time walking willingly into the lion's den. I had honed the ability to detach, to play a role, long ago. Survival often depended on it.

Still, my heart hammered as I let myself in. Cassius was seated on a settee, clad only in a silk robe. He looked up in surprise, his expression quickly shifting to one of interest as he took in my appearance.

"Well, aren't you a tasty little morsel," he said, all but drooling, sizing me up with a glint in his eye. "To what do I owe the pleasure?"

I fluttered my lashes, all innocence and spice. "Madame thought you deserved a treat," I purred, laying the bait.

His lips curved into a satisfied smile. "Did she now? Remind me to thank her later." He leaned back, hands clasped behind his head. "Well then, my dear, why don't you show me what hidden talents you possess.

I sashayed over to the wine like it was a lover I hadn't seen in a decade. "Perhaps we should loosen up a bit first," I suggested, pouring two glasses of the rich Valpolicella. I handed one to Cassius and cozied up next to him on the settee, like a cat ready to purr its way into his lap. He eagerly clinked his glass to mine.

"To new acquaintances." He took a long draw of the wine, eyes never leaving me. I pretended to sip, watching as he quickly drained his glass. The wine would help relax inhibitions, make him more malleable.

"So what brings a lovely thing like you to Madame Velvetine's?" Cassius asked. "You're far too exotic a flower to be wilting away in a place like this."

I offered him a smile spicy enough to start a fire. "We all have our reasons, don't we? What matters isn't where we come from, but where the night takes us."

He chuckled. "Too right, my dear," he said, thrusting his glass at me for another round. "And your name was...?"

I refilled his wine, the dark liquid swirling hypnotically. "Names have power. Tonight, I'm whoever your heart desires me to be."

Cassius' eyes gleamed with lust. "A woman of mystery. I like that." He shifted closer, the sickly-sweet wine heavy on his breath. "I have so many desires racing through my heart right now. Why don't you help me sort through them?"

I let my fingers trail lightly up his arm. "First, let's loosen you up a bit more. I want you completely relaxed and open to...possibilities."

I reached for the wine bottle again, pouring him a third glass. Cassius drank deeply, seeming to forget my presence for a moment as he savored the rich flavors. His cheeks were flushed, eyes heavy-lidded. Perfect.

Setting the glass down, I moved behind him and began massaging his shoulders, kneading firmly. "So tell me, Cassius, what passions drive a man like you?"

He moaned appreciatively at my ministrations. "Other than fine wine and the company of beguiling creatures like yourself? Sadly, little brings me joy these days."

"Come now," I nudged, my hands working magic on his flesh. "An intelligent man like you must have some intriguing pursuits. Does your work not provide stimulation?"

Cassius snorted. "My work? Nothing but ledgers and

accounts. And in fact, I'll need you to really work out these knots. I've been under immense pressure."

"I'm here to make it all better," I cooed, gesturing to the massage table. "If would like to disrobe and lie face down, I can begin properly."

As Cassius got naked, a tightness seized my chest. One misstep and this charade would collapse, putting not just myself but Amelia and perhaps even others I cared for at even more risk. Thomas's words echoed in my mind.

I shook my head sharply, banishing the image of Thomas's ocean-blue eyes and the feeling of his hand against my cheek. There was no room for doubt, not when I was so close to bringing Stanton's empire crumbling down. Thomas could no longer stomach the investigation but he didn't understand—the authorities were powerless against Stanton. If I didn't act, no one would.

Cassius clearing his throat brought me back to the present. He was sprawled on the massage table, a massive tangle of muscle and sinew. I poured oil into my palms and began kneading the tension from his shoulders. Cassius groaned.

"Rough week?" I asked lightly, my hands doing the tango down his spine.

"You could say that," Cassius grumbled into the headrest. "My boss is incredibly demanding. All the money I make lining his pockets, you'd think he'd cut me some slack."

I made an encouraging noise, signaling Cassius to continue venting while my mind whirred.

"Doesn't trust anyone," Cassius went on bitterly. "Breathing down my neck day and night. 'More profits, Cassius! Faster, Cassius!' No appreciation for the risks I take to keep his books balanced."

I leaned heavier into a knot below his shoulder blade. "That sounds incredibly stressful. I had no idea how much responsibility you shouldered."

Cassius huffed out a harsh laugh. "You think he could keep all those enterprises running without me? I know every client, every transaction. Not that the old miser shows any gratitude."

My pulse quickened but I kept my touch steady, not wanting to spook him.

"Impressive. It must take someone incredibly smart to manage such a complex web," I marveled, infusing my voice with awe. "I can't imagine the burdens you carry. You clearly handle massive amounts of money."

I felt Cassius tense under my fingers. Had I pushed too far? I held my breath, kneading his shoulders in silence, letting him turn over the conversation himself.

Finally, he spoke, his gravelly voice low. "It's not easy. The old money trails, hidden accounts, laundering schemes...I keep it locked up tight as a drum. Wouldn't want that kind of information leaking out."

I trailed my fingers down his spine. "Of course. You're obviously a man of discretion. I can't fathom the details involved in managing a complex financial network." I leaned down to murmur in his ear. "You must be absolutely brilliant."

Cassius shivered at my warm breath on his skin. When he replied, there was a hint of pride in his tone. "I do have a knack for the numbers game. Memorized all the ins and outs of Stanton's hoard. Not that anyone appreciates the intricacy involved."

I was close, I could feel it. "I appreciate it," I purred. "In fact, I'm fascinated by the challenge of managing assets on such an immense scale. It sounds incredibly complex, far beyond an ordinary person's capabilities."

I sensed Cassius's mind go into overdrive, no doubt wondering whether he should clam up, and realized I needed a further distraction. I needed him to trust me.

"Flip over onto your back," I said, continuing the massage as he complied. "You're so tense. Let me really work these knots out."

Cassius groaned appreciatively as I kneaded the tight muscles along his shoulders, then paused, giving him an appraising look.

"You know, I'd really be able to do a better job if I wasn't so restricted. Do you mind if I get a bit more comfortable?"

Cassius raised an eyebrow, a glint in his eye. "By all means, get as comfortable as you like."

Cassius's eyes were locked on me, his gaze burning. I took my time, savoring the moment, teasing him with slow, deliberate movements.

I loosened the laces at the back of my dress until the fabric hung loosely from my shoulders. I traced my fingers over the intricate lacework around the collar, feeling a thrill run through me as Cassius's breath caught in his throat. And then, I let the dress drop, inch-by-inch, one finger pulling ever so slowly to reveal a nipple as his breath caught, then the entirety of my bare chest, my under-breast corset tightly hugging my body. It was a necessity to hide the telltale rib bandages from my recent injury, but it also happened to accentuate my curves in a way that was hard to resist.

I could feel the burning intensity of Cassius's desire in the way he looked at me. His eyes locked onto my exposed breasts, a mixture of longing and passion in his gaze. My nipples hardened as if on cue under his intense scrutiny.

His gaze lingered on the curve where my breasts met the corset, and I could see the desire in his eyes as he imagined running his hands over my sensitive skin. It was as if he wanted nothing more than to bury his face between my breasts and taste every inch of their sweet flesh.

"Please, tell me more about all the work stress you've been holding in. Let it all out. Keeping all those secrets bottled up is bad for your health," I purred, leaning in to resume the massage.

His eyes stayed locked on my breasts as I allowed him a closer look.

"Perhaps I could confess a few details," he conceded, a new roughness in his voice. "Just to ease my mind."

I nodded. "That's it. Confess all your sins and absolve yourself, handsome."

I massaged my way to his chest and as my hands glided

over his skin, I could feel the tension melting away. His muscles relaxed beneath my touch, and his breathing deepened. It was a seductive dance, and one that I knew how to play with the best of them.

I moved down his body slowly, each touch sending shivers through him. When I reached his thighs, I paused for a moment, letting my fingers linger just long enough to make him squirm. Then, with a sly grin, I continued until I reached his groin.

Cassius moaned softly as my fingers traced the outline of his erection through the thin sheet covering him.

His eyes fluttered shut as he surrendered to the pleasure of my touch.

"Unburden yourself, handsome," I whispered, as I added more oil to my hands and removed the sheet, grasping his cock.

Information began to flow like water from a dam that had been breached. Little bits at first, and then more.

"The core is the ledgers," he gasped as I slowly worked him to full hardness. "Every transaction, every client...recorded in those books."

I had to admit, it wasn't just the information that had me hooked, it was the way Cassius responded to me. His body trembled beneath my hands as I massaged him. It was intoxicating - the power that flowed through me as I controlled this man with nothing but my touch and wit was unlike anything else. And as we continued our dance of seduction and manipulation, I knew that we were getting closer and closer to uncovering Stanton's secrets once and for all.

But my distraction must have alerted him to something and he started to come out of the trance, possibly second-guessing what he had divulged. I quickly brought my nipple to his lips as I continued to stroke him, and he went back under my trance, sucking eagerly like a starving man feasting on a meal long overdue.

My fingers wrapped harder around Cassius's erection, stroking him with a firm grip that made his whole body tense. His breath quickened as I increased the pace, my thumb gliding over the sensitive head with each stroke. The room filled with the sound of his ragged breathing and my own soft, encouraging murmurs.

Cassius moaned softly, his eyes fluttering shut as he surrendered to the pleasure building within him. "I can't take much more."

I smiled wickedly, knowing that I had him right where I wanted him. "Just a little bit more," I whispered, my voice low and seductive. "You'll never be at ease if you don't unburden yourself fully." His body trembled beneath my touch as he hesitated for a moment, the brink of orgasm teetering precariously close. I paused, stopping my strokes.

"Please," he begged. "Don't stop."

"You'll only be unburdened if you let go of all your secrets," I said, teasing the head of his cock with another, gentle flick of my thumb.

And then, with a sigh almost of defeat, he let slip the location of a hidden safe containing Stanton's ledgers.

"The bakery…" he panted, his voice hoarse with desire. "Toffino's…in the safe."

I could feel my heart racing as I listened to his confession. I'd finally found what I was looking for.

I grabbed his cock hard, stroking my full gratitude at his divulgence and as Cassius reached his climax, spilling himself into my hand in a hot rush of pleasure, I felt a thrill of triumph. His body trembled and shuddered, lost in ecstasy even as he betrayed his boss's secrets to me.

A part of me thrilled at the power I held over him in that moment, reducing this man to a whimpering, quivering mess with the touch of my hand. But even as I reveled in my victory, I couldn't ignore a twisting in my gut.

Pity. Shame.

My methods, though successful, left a bitter taste. And as I cleaned my hands and got dressed, I remembered Thomas's sad gaze. But it was too late for regret. I had to see this through.

I slipped through the still-quiet streets, my footsteps

echoing off the cobblestones. After a quick stop at home, my wee-hours destination was the small, unassuming bakery on the edge of the city that Cassius—bless his loose lips—had revealed to me. My pulse quickened as I approached. This was it—my chance to finally gain hard evidence against Stanton and his band of merry assholes.

I reached the bakery and found the front door predictably locked. Luckily, I had come prepared. Crouching down, I pulled out my lockpick tools and whispered sweet nothings to that ancient hunk of iron until it clicked open. Within seconds, the ancient iron lock gave way with a soft click. I slowly turned the handle and eased the door open, wincing as it creaked louder than my grandma's knees. So much for subtlety.

Inside, I found myself surrounded by the comforting smells of fresh bread and sugar. No time for foodgasms, though—I had a job to do. I made my way between the long wooden tables to the back. Sure enough, tucked behind a large painting of Stanton himself—how original—was a wall safe.

My pulse quickened. This was it.

I retrieved a stethoscope from my bag and got busy cracking the combination. The faint clicks echoed in my ears as I turned the dial, listening for the telltale click. After a few minutes, the final gear slid into place. Holding my breath, I turned the handle and was rewarded with a satisfying clunk as the heavy door swung open.

Inside was a single leather-bound ledger. I reverently lifted it out, hardly daring to believe this might be the evidence I needed. With slightly shaky hands, I opened it, revealing row after row of numbers, dates, and names in faded ink. Flipping through the pages, I caught references to accounts, payments, and what looked like code words for illegal activities. This was it—the key to unraveling Stanton's web of lies, corruption, and douchebaggery.

My mind raced as I tried to decipher connections between people, places, and events mentioned in the ledger. If I could just work it all out, I might finally be able to connect the dots and expose the truth for all to see.

I forced myself to close the ledger and secure it in my bag. I needed to cover my tracks. Meticulously, I spun the safe's combination and after one final visual sweep to ensure everything looked undisturbed, I slipped out of the bakery, carefully easing the door shut behind me.

I stuck to the shadows as I swiftly made my way back through the winding streets. My pulse was racing, but my mind was clear and focused. With the information from the ledger, perhaps Stanton's cruel reign could finally be brought to an end.

By the time I returned home, the city was rubbing the sleep from its eyes, and I, with that ledger snug in my bag, was about to give it a hell of a wake-up call. Shopkeepers threw open their doors, and I took a deep breath, feeling the optimism swell within me. Today just might be the dawn of a new era.

Exhausted after my late-night escapades, I was still asleep hours later when a thunderous pounding shattered the early-afternoon calm. Before I could so much as reply with a particularly scathing insult, the front door burst open, the wood splintering from the force. My blood turned to ice as I found myself face-to-face with a half dozen men, led by none other than Cassius himself.

For a split second, we stared at each other, then Cassius' face twisted into a malicious sneer. "We meet again," he sneered, as if he'd rehearsed it in front of a mirror. Cute.

My mind raced, calculating options for escape, but I was trapped. Cassius' hulking men moved to block every exit, hands hovering ominously over concealed weapons. How had they found me?

Cassius prowled toward me like a predator circling wounded prey. "Did you really think your little deception would go unnoticed?" he taunted.

I clenched my fists, ready to spit venom. "I don't know what you're talking about," I said evenly.

Cassius let out a sharp laugh. "Oh, come now, let's not play games."

I cursed myself for not being more careful. Victoria Caldwell had probably found my shop days ago, and after they all realized what had gone down, fed the info to Cassius. But there was no way in hell I was giving Cassius the satisfaction of a confession. "I suggest you and your men leave before things get ugly."

Cassius stepped closer until his face was just inches from mine, his hot breath assaulting my senses. "Poor, naive Elizabeth," he oozed like a slug. "Did you really think you could waltz in and steal from one of the most dangerous men in the city without consequence?"

My hands curled into fists, every muscle taut and ready to strike. I stared him down unflinchingly. "I serve a higher purpose than your crooked boss ever will. Now get out of my home."

Suddenly, Cassius struck me hard across the face. My head jerked to the side, spots flashing across my vision. Before I could recover, two of his thugs grabbed my arms in vice-like grips. I thrashed against them, but their hold was unbreakable.

Cassius straightened his coat with a casual air. "You've caused quite the disruption to Lord Stanton's affairs. He doesn't take kindly to meddlers." He drew a pistol from his belt, casually turning it over in his hands. "You really should have learned to mind your own business."

Fear surged through me at the sight of the gun, but still I held Cassius' gaze defiantly. "Anything that threatens the innocent becomes my business," I growled.

Cassius shook his head in mock regret. "Oh Miss Templeton, your bleeding heart will be your undoing." He leveled the pistol at my chest. "But don't worry, your martyrdom will be swift."

My pulse roared in my ears. So, this was how it would end - shot dead in my own house by Stanton's lackeys. I couldn't help but think about Amelia, and how I'd let her down. I tensed, ready to face my fate with courage.

Suddenly, the air exploded with noise and chaos. The window shattered as a brick came hurtling through as if delivered by the postal service from hell, catching one of the thugs holding me square in the head. As he crumpled, the grip on my arm loosened just enough for me to wrench free. I drove my elbow back into my second captor's gut then whipped around to deliver a swift uppercut to his jaw that laid him out flat.

Cassius swore as he swiveled the gun toward the broken window. But quick as a flash, I launched myself forward and delivered a roundhouse kick that sent the pistol skittering across the floor. We both dove for it, colliding painfully as we scrambled desperately.

But just as victory was in my grasp, the click of another gun cocking was louder than my own cursed thoughts.

"Don't move," came a gruff voice.

I froze, Cassius going still beside me. The heavy tread of boots approached as I realized with sinking dread that Cassius' men had me surrounded. Rough hands grabbed my shoulders, hauling me to my feet.

Before I could react, a cloth was pressed over my nose and mouth, cloying fumes overwhelming my senses. I managed a few clumsy swings before my limbs grew leaden and darkness crept into my vision. The last thing I saw before descending into oblivion was Cassius' snarling face, twisted in triumph.

And then my world went black.

Chapter 13

Consciousness came in slow, hazy waves. I drifted in and out, unable to grasp onto full awareness. Snippets flashed through my mind - rough hands grabbing at me, the ground lurching beneath my feet, Cassius' face contorted into a grin that could curdle milk. But the images slipped away like smoke before I could make sense of them.

The first concrete sensation I registered was pain. A bone-deep throbbing that seemed to pulse through every fiber of my body. I tried to move, only for the ache to sharpen into daggers of fire. A low groan escaped my throat.

"Elizabeth? Oh thank Christ, you're awake."

Oliver's face swam into view, all furrowed brows and worry lines. I blinked slowly, trying to shake off the clinging fog in my mind. The room swam into focus, and I was grateful to see that it was my own. Thank fuck for small miracles.

"What the hell happened?" I rasped, my tongue feeling thick and clumsy in my mouth.

Oliver's expression turned grave. "You were attacked. When I came to open the bookshop this morning, I saw some brutes forcing their way into your flat. I ran for the police, and they were coming, but..." His round face crumpled even more. "I'm sorry, I threw a brick through your window to distract them. They finally scattered as the police arrived. We found you unconscious on the floor."

The memories hit me like a runaway carriage - Cassius, the struggle, the smell of the rag with its scent like it had been marinated in Satan's armpit. I stiffened, panic shooting through me.

I lifted a hand to gingerly probe at my face, wincing. Cassius and his thugs had done a number on me, no doubt about that. But I knew they hadn't gotten their hands on the evidence. A quick glace told me my hiding place was still secure.

Before I could grill Ollie for more details, heavy footsteps sounded from down the hall. I braced myself.

Thomas's tall frame filled the doorway a moment later, his handsome face creased in a ferocious scowl. His piercing eyes raked over my battered form, fury smoldering in their depths.

"I'll give you a moment," Oliver murmured tactfully before slipping from the room.

Thomas crossed to the bed in two long strides and crouched down, bringing his face level with mine. His big hands, normally so deft and gentle, shook with barely suppressed rage as he reached to cup my cheek.

"Who did this to you?" he demanded, his voice low and dangerous.

I quickly relayed the whole confrontation with Cassius and his thugs, watching as Thomas's face went from stormy to apocalyptic, his jaw clenched so hard I thought it might snap. "I'm going to kill them for laying a hand on you," he growled.

Despite everything, his protectiveness made warmth spark in my chest. But I knew his anger came from more than just what had happened today.

"Thomas..." I began gently.

But he barreled on as if I hadn't spoken, his voice becoming more agitated. "This has gone too far, Elizabeth. You need to stop before..." His throat bobbed as he struggled to continue. "Before the next time I find you, it's in the morgue."

I wanted to soothe away the anguish written plainly across his handsome face. But I knew if I tried to tell him I would be fine, that I could handle Stanton and his goons, it would only spark an argument. Thomas cared too much to look at this rationally.

Instead, I reached for his hand, clasping it weakly in my own. "I know you're scared," I said softly. "But please, trust me. I can't walk away now."

He let out a shaky breath, turning his head aside. We sat in silence for a long moment, hands entwined, as I hoped he would understand.

Finally, Thomas met my eyes again, jaw set in resignation. "You're the most stubborn woman I've ever met, you know that?" He tried for a teasing tone, but his voice was heavy with suppressed emotion.

I gave him a faint smile. "It's part of my charm."

His answering chuckle was strained, but it seemed the storm had passed. He gently squeezed my fingers.

"When I gave you that ultimatum the other night, I truly thought it would stop you. I never imagined you'd go off all on your own and..." His voice trailed off, his face a battle ground of emotion as he seemed to come to a decision. "...I can see now that you're not going to stop, no matter what the cost. I should have known trying to control the situation would only make it worse."

I nodded. Last night, all of it had only hardened my resolve.

He let out a hard sigh. "As much as it hurts to see you like this, I can't let you continue alone. I don't want you to do this, but if you won't give up, then I want to help you. But no more secrets."

A pang of guilt shot through me as his piercing gaze bore into me, full of sincerity. "We'll take down Stanton together."

I knew I couldn't refuse him. Thomas was a part of this, whether I liked it or not. And I had to admit, with his keen mind and dogged determination, he would be a valuable asset.

Slowly, I nodded. Thomas let out a breath, his rigid posture relaxing slightly.

"Okay," I agreed softly. "Together."

A small, bittersweet smile crossed his lips. But before he could reply, Oliver bustled back into the room bearing a tray.

"I've brought some broth, the perfect restorative," he pronounced, setting it on the bedside table with a flourish.

Despite the lingering ache in my bones, I realized I was

ravenous. With Thomas' help, I managed to prop myself up on the pillows.

By the time I drained the last drops of broth, exhaustion was threatening to pull me back under. Thomas gently eased me down onto the pillows again, brushing a stray curl back from my forehead with a touch so tender it made my heart clench.

"Get some rest," he murmured. "We can continue planning our next steps when you're stronger."

I wanted to protest that I was fine, but my traitorous eyelids were already slipping closed. As I hovered on the edge of sleep, I felt the light press of lips against my hair.

"Sweet dreams, Elizabeth," Thomas' voice whispered through the gathering fog in my mind. Then I let the darkness take me, feeling safe and protected in a way I hadn't in longer than I could remember.

Later that night, Thomas came back to strategize. Wordlessly, I moved to the corner of the room, pushing aside the false panel to reveal my hidden workspace. Logs, ledgers, and maps littered the table, the web I had been meticulously spinning to unravel Stanton's far-reaching empire.

"Well, Miss Templeton, you never cease to amaze me," Thomas said, coaxing a smile from me.

"I thought," I began, "that once I got the ledger, it would be over. Until the ledger itself told me that half the police force is under Stanton's control. So many more than we imagined."

Thomas nodded. "So we can't trust anyone."

I shook my head and we fell into a heavy silence, then poured over every scrap of intel, looking for weaknesses to exploit. The candlelight flickered shadows across our faces as we traced lines and figures with our fingers, mentally calculating how to bring the corrupt behemoth crashing down. The room was silent except for the whisper of turning pages and the scratching of pens.

Thomas's eyes gleamed as his fingers danced across the ledger, plotting financial ruin. When it came to numbers and strategy, he was in his element. While Thomas devised an economic offensive, my mind turned to more personal tactics. Stanton himself had to be the primary target. Without the head, the body would wither.

"I could get close to him through Caldwell," I mused. Thomas's head jerked up, his body tensing like I'd suggested a skinny-dip in the Thames.

"Absolutely not. Elizabeth, that's suicide," he argued vehemently.

I held up a hand to stem his protests. "Just hear me out. You're too recognizable to get into his inner circle unnoticed. But I still have contacts, allies. I can get access."

Thomas's jaw clenched, the muscles rippling. When he spoke, his voice was tight with restraint.

"Need I remind you what he's capable of? What he's already done? What Caldwell has already don?" His eyes bored into mine, willing me to reconsider. But my mind was set.

"I appreciate your concern. But neither of us got where we are by playing it safe." I kept my voice firm but gentle.

"God dammit," Thomas said, and then an unspoken understanding passed between us.

We would drive ourselves mad trying to dissuade the other from danger. It was a fight that could never be won.

Thomas closed his eyes and let out a slow breath. When he opened them, the protests had been neatly tucked away, replaced by steely resolve.

"Just promise me you'll be careful," was all he said.

I gave him a small smile.

A memory surfaced unbidden - Amelia's face the last time I had seen her, her eyes full of fear but also hope. Hope that I could help her escape the clutches of the man who had caused her such pain. That man who sat atop an empire built on the backs of the weak. Inaction - allowing Stanton's web to grow unchecked - was its own kind of violence.

Across from me, Thomas nodded slowly as if reading my thoughts. Our eyes met in silent understanding.

I squeezed Thomas's hand, taking comfort in its solid warmth.

The mood lightened as we lost ourselves in logistics, taking solace in the methodical planning of sabotage.

Finally, as the night stretched to the wee hours, we were ready. Thomas rose and donned his coat, the game set in motion. He moved to the doorway but hesitated before leaving. In three long strides he crossed the room and pulled me into a crushing embrace.

"Be safe, I'll see you tomorrow," he whispered into my hair and then he vanished, his footsteps a ghost's whisper in the hall.

Alone in the dim room, I sank down on the narrow cot I kept in the hidden room and closed the panel to seal myself in, in case anyone decided to come back for me.

Tomorrow I would become someone else, shedding my skin for a new identity once again. Tonight, I allowed myself simply to be.

I snuffed out the last candle and curled up beneath the blankets. As the first tendrils of sleep wrapped around me, I sent up a silent prayer to whatever forces might be listening. Keep them all safe - Amelia, Thomas, Jacob.

The lantern's dying light threw patterns of shadows across the walls. Then, darkness took me.

Chapter 14

The next evening, the pounding of my heart threatened to drown out the muted conversations around me as I entered the lavish foyer.

My eyes darted, taking in the opulent surroundings - ornate moldings, glittering chandeliers, gentlemen in tailcoats and ladies dripping in silks and jewels. It was everything I expected from one of high society's elite gatherings, and yet its grandeur only intensified the knot in my stomach.

I smoothed my hands over the rich satin of my gown, the color of a fine Merlot. The dark wig I wore itched like a motherfucker but I resisted the urge to scratch, keeping my spine stiff and expression neutral. Heavy stage makeup helped obscure my identity. Combined with an assumed name and fabricated background story, I felt reasonably confident I could maintain the ruse.

My fingers drifted absently to the delicate golden chain around my neck, fingertips tracing the intricate locket that hung at its end. A nervous habit I couldn't seem to shake. To any onlooker it would appear a piece of jewelry and nothing more. But within the locket's enameled casing lay something far more precious - a tiny vial filled with clear liquid.

My ticket to getting the information I needed out of the elusive Lord Stanton.

Intel said he would be in attendance tonight. My eyes swept the crowded room, scanning for my target. No sign of his domineering presence yet. I exhaled slowly, willing my nerves to settle. Patience. I could be patient.

I moved farther into the room with measured steps, mimicking the practiced grace of the ladies around me. Chin up, back straight, smile in place but not too broad. The image of poise and manners, betraying none of the adrenaline charging through my veins.

Years of assuming false identities had honed my ability to blend in, to become someone new, shedding myself like a snake shedding its skin. It was freeing, in a way, to take on these personas. I could be anyone but me. No messy past, no teetering pile of regrets. Just a clean slate.

Tonight, I was Adaline Duval, mystic extraordinaire, a spiritualist with a direct line to otherworldly realms. My role was to provide the evening's entertainment, capturing the imagination and gossip of those around me. The perfect guise to get close to Stanton.

A high, tinkling laugh drew my attention and I turned to find a small gathering of ladies eyeing me with unabashed interest. Their vibrant silks and dripping jewels rustled as they leaned in close to each other, already whispering behind their lace fans. Word of the mysterious newcomer had clearly spread.

Time to give them a show.

I glided over with a serene smile. "Good evening, ladies. I don't believe we've had the pleasure of an introduction just yet."

The brunette in the center, clearly their ringleader, extended a gloved hand. "Lady Eunice Johnston, what a delight to make your acquaintance." Her smile didn't reach her pale eyes but her voice dripped with enough honey to attract all the bees. "The others and I were just dying to meet the newest member of society, especially one as…intriguing as yourself."

The embellished inflection on that last word was not lost on me. These women wanted a spectacle and I would deliver.

I met Lady Johnston's gaze evenly. "Adaline Duval, charmed I'm sure. I can't imagine what rumors might be swirling about little old me."

A delicate titter passed between the women. The game was

on.

"Come now, Mrs. Duval, a woman of your talents should wear them proudly," Johnston purred, her curiosity poorly veiled. "We heard you were something of a psychic."

I arched one penciled brow. "Among other things."

This elicited another round of titters and fervent whispering behind fans. Johnston's smile broadened, showing the barest hint of teeth. There was an almost predatory glint in her eyes now.

"How thrilling! You simply must tell us our fortunes." The request sounded more like a command. Clearly, she was used to getting her way.

But I needed to keep these peacocks occupied and their attention on me. I gestured for the ladies to gather in, as if sharing coy secrets just between us girls. They complied eagerly, silk skirts brushing against mine in a rainbow of colors.

Up close I could see the layers of powder and rouge masking their features, setting them apart from the natural beauty of youth.

Ms. Johnston extended her hand expectantly. "Shall we start with me?"

I gave a serene smile. "But of course."

Grasping her slim fingers lightly in mine, I let my eyes drift half-closed, as if focusing some inner sight. I felt Lady Johnston lean closer, her breath catching slightly in anticipation. The others followed suit, practically buzzing with intrigue.

Time to craft some convincing fortune-telling that revealed little but hinted at everything. I'd found most people's imaginations supplied all the details if fed even the barest crumbs to spur them on. And judging by this crowd, their imaginations were feasting tonight.

"Mmmm..." I murmured, lowering my voice an octave. "I see...power. You seek control, over yourself and those around you. But take care that pride does not blind ambition. Only by opening your eyes to another's perspective will you find the fulfillment you crave." I lifted my eyes to Johnston's, giving her hand a delicate squeeze. "Do not fear change, but welcome growth, and your rewards shall be great."

I released her hand and leaned back, watching as she processed my words, a small furrow between her brows. Murmurs rippled through her companions, no doubt dissecting my cryptic message in their own way, finding snippets to fuel gossip. Johnston remained silent, eyes distant in contemplation. I hid a smile. The hook was set.

I turned to the next lady, taking her proffered hand. "And for you, my dear..."

I continued on down the line, delivering similarly vague fortunes in a breathy, mystical tone, hinting at whatever desires these ladies clung to most fiercely - power, status, beauty, secrets. Their eyes lit up in turn as I hit my marks, whispering behind their hands in delight.

Soon I felt Johnston's considering gaze on me once more. "You are the real thing, Mrs. Duval, such insight! You simply must tell me who I'll be married to next. This widow business does grow tiresome."

Her companions tittered but I caught the sharp look that passed between them. She had revealed a vulnerability I could use.

I took her hand again, turning it palm up, and made a show of studying the lines there. My voice dropped low, as if imparting profound wisdom meant only for her.

"Marriage is but a stepping stone on life's path, not the destination. True partnership lies in seeing another fully and accepting unconditionally. Only then will you find one worthy of standing at your side when all other finery fades away. Look not with your eyes but your heart, and you will know their face as well as your own."

I pressed my fingertip to her palm for emphasis before releasing her hand. Caldwell sat silent, gaze turned inward once more. The other ladies squirmed with thinly veiled curiosity but didn't dare break the contemplative spell that had fallen over her.

I hid a satisfied smirk. Give a person something to chew on and their mind would conjure a whole feast. Fortune told, I made my excuses and slipped away from the clucking hens, leaving them to hem and haw over the meaning of my words.

As I moved through the crowded ballroom, I kept one eye trained for any sign of Stanton's arrival. But the sea of glittering dresses and tailcoats revealed nothing. It seemed the elusive Lord kept late hours. Very well. I would bide my time. Blend in. Wait for my opening. Patience was a skill finely honed out of necessity. I could be patient.

Over the next hour, I caught Thomas's eye several times, and each time he sent me the tiniest hint of a smile, letting me know he was there if I needed anything, but what I needed most was simply his presence, especially once Stanton arrived.

Finally, all eyes turned toward the ornate doors as they swung open. A hush fell over the crowd as Stanton strode into the room, chin lifted with arrogant confidence. He cut an elegant figure in his tailored suit, but his striking silver hair and piercing gaze marked him unmistakably as a man accustomed to power. And fear.

His presence seemed to suck the air from the room. I felt hundreds of spines stiffen and pulses quicken as he passed through the parted crowd. No one wished to catch his eye or the attention of his entourage of stone-faced guards. Iron fists hidden beneath velvet gloves - that was Stanton's way.

As the doors swung shut behind him with an ominous thud, the music and chatter resumed, perhaps a bit more shrill and forced than before. Stanton paid no mind, already commanding a circle of sycophants vying for his favor.

Steeling my resolve, I began to thread through the crowd toward my prey. My hands trembled faintly as I reached for the vial of serum tucked into my pendant necklace. Iris, a former associate and the serum's creator, had warned me not to waste a precious drop. "The tongue becomes loosened but focus quickly fades," she had cautioned. I needed to keep Stanton lucid long enough to learn what I needed. It was a dangerous high-wire act, but it was time to drag his misdeeds into the light.

As I neared Stanton's circle, I swept my shaking hands down the front of my gown, smoothing away any hint of anxiety. I would need to charm the snake if I wanted to slip past its fangs.

I insinuated myself next to a lady clutching a tiny dog, providing the perfect pretext. "Oh, what an adorable little creature!" I cooed. "He simply reminds me of the darling Duchess Rothschild's Pom, Belladonna. Have you had the pleasure of making the Duchess's acquaintance?"

I continued nattering about the Duchess loud enough to catch Stanton's attention. As planned, he turned with thinly veiled annoyance at the interruption. Perfect. His irritation left him open, willing to grasp at any new diversion from the simpering flock surrounding him.

I turned my gaze upon Stanton, arranging my face into an expression of modest pleading. "Forgive my intrusion, Lord Stanton, but I simply had to make your acquaintance this evening.

I dropped into a low curtsy, holding his gaze. " Adaline Duval, my lord. I have heard such astonishing tales of your...interests." I let my voice breathlessly trail off.

Stanton appraised me with a predator's eye, no doubt taking in my low décolletage. Good. His interest was caught. Now to reel him in.

"You have quite the spirit, Madam," he said, giving me a slight nod.

I smiled brightly, gently worrying my pendant between my fingers, watching Stanton's gaze follow the motion. His dark eyes glinted with discernible hunger as they traced the curves the necklace drew attention to. How predictable men were in their desires. Useful, but predictable.

"In fact, spirit is exactly the right word for I do have some expertise in the area of the spirit world," I continued lightly. "I would be honored to give you a private demonstration, if you wished."

Stanton considered me a moment more before inclining his head. "A demonstration does sound...intriguing. Lead the way, Miss Duval."

"Perhaps a few of us could make a small audience," Thomas swiftly chimed in from where he had been loitering nearby. "I'd love a bit of a show," he said, smiling that charming smile of his that made ladies woozy and had men wishing they could be him.

"Please, be my guest," Stanton said, looking Thomas up and down, no doubt sizing him up as a potential future business associate.

The circle of aristocrats parted as I led Stanton and the others from the ballroom down a darkened corridor. The murmurs and music faded the further we walked, matching the quickening of my pulse. We reached a small parlor where I had staged everything necessary for an enthralling séance.

I lit the candles with a flourish, their flickering light casting ominous shadows about the room. The table was set with a cloth, cards, crystals and other accoutrements to set the mood. Two glasses and a breathing bottle of deep red wine stood at the ready. I glanced at Stanton to gauge his reaction.

His expression remained neutral, but a gleam of interest shone in his eyes. Good. I pulled out a chair and beckoned him to sit across from me. He settled into the seat, long fingers tapping expectantly on the table. It was time to begin the show.

I closed my eyes, letting my breathing slow. When I opened my them, I let their focus drift, as if seeing beyond this plane of existence.

"Welcome, Lord Stanton," I intoned, my voice low. "The spirits have longed for your presence this evening."

I waved my hands over the table, letting my movements grow more frenetic. "I sense a presence here with us now, seeking to make contact..."

I allowed my voice to tremble, glancing anxiously about the room. Stanton watched me intently, leaning forward in anticipation. Good, his skepticism was fading. Time to reel him in further.

I gasped loudly. "Yes, I see her now. A lady, regal in bearing and dress. She says her name is...Lady Anna?" I glanced at Stanton for confirmation.

His eyes widened fractionally. "My late mother's name, yes. Can you really see her?"

A murmur went through the small crowd. I nodded, letting a look of serene calm settle on my features. "She is here with us and wishes to speak with you."

I picked up the wine with care, pouring us each a glass while surreptitiously unstopping the vial at my throat and performing a little sleight of hand as I passed Stanton his glass. "A toast, to welcome the spirits," I proclaimed. Our glasses met with a melodic chime.

Stanton took a long draught as I pretended to sip. In truth, I did not let a single drop pass my lips. I needed my wits intact for what was to come.

Setting my glass down, I closed my eyes again, swaying gently in my seat. "Oh yes, I can feel Lady Anna drawing closer now. She wishes to relay a message..."

I settled deeper into the role of conduit, letting my voice shift and tremble as I invented an exchange between Stanton and his dead mother. In truth, it didn't matter what she supposedly said, so long as it kept Stanton engaged. I simply needed to buy time for the serum to take effect.

Gradually, I let my words grow more probing. "Lady Anna says there are secrets you keep buried away, even from yourself. Painful memories you've tried to forget."

I paused just enough to see Stanton shift in discomfort. The serum was working. His true spirit was unmooring from its cage of lies. Now to direct its course with care.

"She implores you - speak the truth you have locked away so long. Let your soul be unburdened," I implored, infusing my voice with warmth and compassion.

Stanton's eyes took on a faraway look. When he spoke, his voice was hoarse, as if pulled from some long-forgotten place. "There are deeds I regret. Things I have done which haunt me still."

It was working. I leaned forward intently, keeping my features soft and open. "Go on. She is here to listen, not to judge."

Stanton wrung his hands, eyes welling with tears. My pulse roared in my ears. This was the moment I'd been waiting for. After so many months of intricate planning, the endgame was within reach. Stanton would condemn himself with his own words, if I could just coax them out.

"I never meant for things to go so far," Stanton murmured. He looked up at me with pleading eyes. "I started off simply wanting justice after my dear mother's senseless murder. But in my grief and rage, I became consumed with vengeance. I went down an increasingly dark path until the man I was became unrecognizable to me."

Stanton's shoulders slumped with the weight of his confession. My entire body hummed with adrenaline, sensing how close revelation hovered. But I needed specifics if I was to expose the full depths of his depravity.

I nodded encouragingly, keeping my voice soft. "Yes, confess your truths so your spirit may find peace. We will listen without judgment. Anna says there is something about..." my eyes blankly searched the air, "...a girl with emerald eyes."

Stanton wrung his hands, clearly fighting an internal battle between secrecy and unburdening. Trapped teetering on the edge of a cliff, and I was ready to give him a gentle push. I held my breath, praying his conscience would win out.

"Yes," he admitted softly. "There is a girl. I've kept her hidden away, in a place where her talents can be properly assessed."

I swallowed, my heart both soaring that Amelia was alive and souring at the revulsion mounting within me. I opened my mouth to press for more details, but suddenly the parlor doors burst open, torn nearly off their hinges by the force. In the doorway stood a figure straight from my nightmares.

Disheveled, with murder blazing in his eyes, stood Cassius. His gaze fixed on me like a hawk spying its prey.

Fear washed over me, cold and absolute.

Chapter 15

Cassius's whisper rippled through the crowd faster than a lit match to kerosene. I watched in numb horror as the gears started turning in the thick skulls of Stanton's men, their faces turning from boredom to alert understanding. The jig was up. My cover had been blown sky high.

My pulse thundered as I quickly weighed my options. I could try to brazen it out, deny everything and hope Cassius didn't have concrete proof. But one look at the suspicious glares and hands reaching into coats told me that wouldn't fly.

I glanced over at Thomas, who looked ready to grab my hand and bolt for the exit. But the briefest shake of my head stopped him short. Thomas's involvement had to remain secret for both our sakes.

"Well, I think we're just about wrapped up here!" I announced like I was the bloody Queen of Sheba. "Thank you all for being such a lovely audience."

I ignored the growing murmurs as I began gathering up my props—a.k.a. stalling—eyes darting around for the fastest escape route. My hands trembled slightly.

I abandoned the equipment and hiked up my skirts, making a break for the side door. Chaos erupted behind me as I dashed into the hallway, shouts and heavy footfalls right on my tail. So much for slipping away unnoticed.

I sprinted down the richly decorated corridor, my satin gown billowing like a bloody parachute. A series of sharp cracks echoed off the walls as a hail of bullets whizzed past, shattering a gilt-framed painting inches from my head.

"Fuck!" I whisper-yelled, dropping into a zig-zag pattern.

Leave it to Stanton's goons to start firing willy-nilly in a crowded party. As I skidded around the corner, another shot zipped by, embedding itself in the silk wallpaper.

On I ran, lungs heaving, the mansion's lavish interiors fading into a blur as I simultaneously prayed to the gods of bad decisions that I would find a way out. Heavy footfalls pounded after me, full of deadly intent.

The shouts grew louder as Stanton's men closed in. I grasped at any tactical advantage, ducking down side passages and vaulting down stairways, using the mansion's maze-like layout to obstruct their pursuit. But they were stubborn bastards.

Up ahead, I spotted an arched window and made a split-second decision. Digging deep, I summoned every last bit of strength and, with the grace of a drunken swan, I launched myself at the windowpane, tucking my body into a tight roll as shards of glass exploded outward.

I hit the gravel walkway hard, grit embedding itself in my palms. No time to worry about that. Ignoring the pain, I wrenched myself to my feet and took off across the gardens. The night air was sweet relief after the chaos inside.

A bloom of warmth spread through the torn silk covering my left bicep. I risked a glance down and swore viciously. The bullet had just grazed me, but blood was already staining the dress's fabric. Nothing fatal, but it stung like hell, though not quite as badly as my ribs.

The shouts behind me were fainter but still too close for comfort. I veered right, aiming for the garden wall shrouded by weeping willows. Scrambling up and over it, I paused for one last look at the grand yard now swarming with Stanton's forces.

With a frustrated huff, I turned my back on the towering edifice and vanished into the dark maze of London's streets. The wound in my arm throbbed angrily, but the adrenaline coursing through me kept the pain at bay. I had to get away first, patch myself up later.

Darting from shadow to shadow, I let my training take over, all senses on high alert as I chose my path seemingly at random, confusing any pursuit. The deserted side streets and alleyways became my domain once again.

My breath wheezed, and my hair tumbled loose from its pins, but I wasn't about to stop, not yet.

I scrambled around a corner into a narrow alley, pressing myself against a rough brick wall as I fought for breath. All was silent except for the frantic pounding of blood in my ears.

Hope bloomed, but caution told me not to rejoice too soon. I forced myself onward through the tangled web of alleys and side streets, sticking to the shadows. My rough escape had carried me deep into the rougher parts of the city, away from the polished world of ballrooms and manners I'd briefly inhabited. Out here, it was everyone for themselves.

Exhaustion seeped into my bones, but I pushed past it, finding refuge in a particularly filthy alley that smelled of piss and broken dreams. My torn gown would blend right into the moldering refuse.

Collapsing against a grimy brick wall, I finally allowed myself a moment of rest, lungs heaving like a racehorse. The oozing wound on my arm burned fiercely now that the rush of adrenaline had faded. I examined it closely, probing the torn edges. Thankfully, the bullet had barely grazed me. It could have been so much worse.

I tore a strip of silk off my once-beautiful gown and wrapped it around the gash, pulling it tight to stem the bleeding. The pressure sent another jolt of pain up my arm, but I gritted my teeth and kept wrapping.

Leaning back against the alley wall, I let the cold brick leach away the frenzied energy that had propelled my escape. My mind reeled back to how the night had ended in chaos. How had Cassius figured it out? I'd been so careful, so meticulous in my act.

But the damage was done.

Stanton knew my face. Granted, what he'd seen was a face with a hell of a lot of makeup, but no amount of rouge or powder could disguise the fact that I'd gone and painted a bullseye on my back.

I couldn't help but worry what that knowledge might mean, how the stakes had ratcheted up to a dangerous new level. The players in this game didn't mess around. And I had just made myself an even bigger target.

Clenching my jaw against a swell of frustration, I pushed away from the wall and the thoughts it harbored. I was too exposed here. Best to get somewhere more secure and regroup. Thomas. I could go to Thomas. He would know what to do next.

The walk to Thomas's home took the last drop of energy from me. By the time his tidy townhouse came into view, I could barely put one foot in front of the other. I slipped down the service alley and knocked softly at the kitchen door. After a long moment, the door swung open, revealing Thomas's beloved face creased with concern.

"Thank God," he breathed, with the fervor of a preacher spying the offertory plate on Sunday, and pulled me swiftly inside. I collapsed into his embrace, breathing in his soothing scent as the events of the night crashed over me.

"Where have you been?" Thomas murmured, his warm hands running gently over me, checking for injuries. "Your arm..."

"It's nothing," I sighed, suddenly feeling the bone-deep exhaustion seeping through my limbs. Adrenaline, it turns out, is not a bottomless well. "Just a scratch."

Thomas's jaw tightened as he examined the clumsy bandage, but he didn't push further.

I let him guide me upstairs to the cozy refuge of his rooms. He carefully unwound the bloodstained scrap of silk from my arm and cleaned the angry wound with a tenderness that made my heart flutter.

"We have to end this, Thomas. We have to get Amelia."

"I know," Thomas said, his voice resolute. "Tomorrow."

The mansion loomed in the distance, a hulking shadow against the night sky. Thomas and I crouched in the underbrush, waiting to make our move. My heart pounded against my ribs and the familiar rush of adrenaline still sang through my veins.

"You good?" Thomas's voice was gravelly, a low rumble that could start landslides or, at the very least, a woman's heart.

I nodded, not trusting my voice to come out steady. We both knew damn well this wasn't my first rodeo, but Thomas liked to play the protector. I'd be lying if I said it didn't warm me up a little inside, so I let him fuss without complaint.

"You really think he's in there?" I asked, hope mingling with dread.

Thomas's jaw tightened. "Jacob seemed sure of it. And that boy hasn't been wrong yet."

I nodded, twisting my fingers together in a rare display of nerves.

Thomas reached over and gave my hand a squeeze. "We've got this, Lizzie. That son of a bitch won't know what hit him."

Despite the graveness of the situation, I smiled. Thomas knew how to steady me.

We sat in silence as the moon disappeared below the horizon, leaving us bathed in the sickly glow of the mansion's lights. It was time. We slipped through the trees as quietly as ghosts, senses on high alert. My cloak swished around my feet and I had to keep pushing my damn curls off my face.

As we crept closer, an unnatural silence enveloped us, thick as clotted cream. My unease grew. Where were the night birds, the hum of insects? It felt like the forest was holding its breath, bracing for violence. Thomas felt it too. I could see it in the set of his shoulders, the tension radiating from him. We were walking right into the lion's den. But it was too late to turn back now.

Pressing my spyglass to my eye, I scanned the mansion, searching for any signs of life. Warm candlelight glowed in many of the windows, but no shadows or movement broke the stillness. Where was everyone?

A twig snapped to our left and we both spun, pistols aimed and ready. Just a rabbit. I released the breath I'd been holding. My heart thundered against my ribs. Dammit, get it together,

Elizabeth.

"I don't like this," Thomas muttered. "Something feels off."

I nodded. Every instinct I had was screaming trap. But the mission came first. If Stanton really was in there, and more importantly Amelia, we had to act now. God only knew what that sick bastard had planned next.

We crept closer, pistols cocked and ready for whatever waited ahead. Thirty yards from the mansion's heavy oak doors, the air shifted somehow, a prelude to mayhem, sending a shiver down my spine like an unwelcome suitor's gaze. The fine hairs on my neck stood at attention. In my periphery, I saw Thomas freeze. He felt it too.

In the span of a heartbeat, the forest came alive. Dark figures poured from the trees, pistols firing.

"Down!" Thomas roared, tackling me behind a fallen tree as lead screamed through the night air.

My shoulder slammed into the ground and all the air rushed from my lungs. Thomas threw himself over me, shielding my body with his. Bullets peppered the earth around us.

"Ambush!" I wheezed out, exhibiting the lung capacity of an asthmatic flea with a smoking problem.

Thomas's eyes blazed with fury. "Goddamn coward," he snarled. "Too afraid to face us head on."

Peering through the not-quite-shield of gnarled roots, I quickly sized up the threat. At least two dozen armed men formed a half circle around our position. We were well and truly pinned down.

Thomas pressed a hand to his side and it came away dark with blood. *Dammit.* He'd been hit. My chest clenched.

"How bad?" I demanded.

"Just a graze," he grunted through gritted teach. "I'll live."

I shook my head, fury rising hot and fast. We should have come yesterday before Stanton had a chance to organize. We'd walked right into his trap. And now Thomas was paying for it.

The gunfire slowed as the shooters paused to reload. Our window. I caught Thomas's eye and saw my own rage mirrored there.

With a roar, we burst from cover, pistols spitting fire and brimstone. Two of Stanton's men dropped before they could train their weapons back on us. We dove behind separate trees, bullets chewing the bark around us.

I took aim at a brute of a man fumbling as he tried to reload. Not on my watch, Sunshine. My pistol sang, and down he went, toppling backward without a sound. One down, too many left to go.

Thomas advanced steadily, popping off rounds like he was born with a gun in his hand instead of a silver spoon. I swelled with pride, and let's face it, another emotion that had no place on a battlefield.

We were outgunned and surrounded, but we would go down fighting. Stanton wanted a war? Oh, I'd give him one alright.

I darted between cover, firing and moving. Bark exploded around me.

Thomas roared and charged toward my position, pistols spitting death. Two more enemies fell beneath his onslaught as he picked up one of their fallen pistols. He was exposed, a perfect target. Fear lanced through me.

"Thomas!"

He whipped around just as a mountain of a man took aim at his back. Thomas dove sideways, but the gunshot roared louder than all the others. A dark blossom spread across Thomas's chest.

"No!" The scream tore from my throat as he stumbled and fell.

Rage like I'd never known flooded my veins, hot as lava. With an animal snarl, I charged from my cover, hurtling toward the brute who'd shot Thomas. He fumbled with his pistol, eyes widening as I descended upon him. My knife flashed in the low light and a crimson slash split his throat.

I stood over him as he gurgled wetly, clutching his

ruined neck. "Rot in hell," I hissed, hardly original under the circumstances but it felt appropriate.

I grabbed the man's gun and spun back toward Thomas.

He was slumped against a tree, pale as a ghost who'd seen a ghost. I sprinted to him just as another bullet split the air by my head, far too close for comfort. Crouching by his side, I quickly assessed the damage. The ball had torn into his shoulder, just above his heart. He was losing blood fast.

Thomas clutched my hand, his grip surprisingly strong despite the pain glazing his eyes.

"Elizabeth, listen to me," he rasped. "Get out of here. It's too late for me but you still have a chance."

"The hell it is," I snarled, ripping fabric from my cloak to bind his wound. "I'm not leaving you."

Gunshots exploded around us like thunder. We were sitting ducks out here. Gritting my teeth, I hoisted Thomas's good arm around my shoulder and dragged him behind a boulder, ignoring his pained groans. He slumped against the rock, face draining of color.

"Why do you have to be so damn stubborn?" he grunted. Despite the situation, his lips quirked in a hint of a smile.

My mind raced, thoughts crashing together in a cacophony of alarm bells. We were trapped, pinned down by gunfire with nowhere to run. I'd led us right into an ambush, too focused on the hunt to consider that we might become the hunted. We were outnumbered, outgunned, and now Thomas was bleeding out right in front of me.

I risked a glance around the tree trunk to assess our situation. A group of shadowy figures were fanned out across the path ahead, cutting off any escape. Their pistols flashed like a deadly fireworks show. I swore creatively under my breath, a string of expletives that would make a sailor blush. We were fish in a barrel.

A wave of dread crashed over me, cold and chilling. I couldn't lose Thomas, not here, not like this. I thought of Amelia's tear-filled eyes as she begged me to take down Stanton, to stop anyone else from enduring the same pain and fear she did. Thomas and I were her only hope. But now, it seemed that hope was fading with each drop of blood that seeped from Thomas's wound.

"Thomas, look at me," I said, summoning every ounce of calm I could fake. "I'm getting you out of here, okay? Just stay with me."

He gave a weak nod, his face ashen. My hands were slick with his blood. Focus, I told myself. Guilt and panic could come later. Right now, survival was all that mattered.

I held my pistol with my left hand, keeping pressure on Thomas's wound with my right. I peered around the tree again, slow and careful, and fired off two quick shots toward the advancing men. My aim was off with my left hand, but it was enough to give them pause. I only needed them to hesitate for a moment.

Before the men could regroup, I hauled Thomas to his feet, pulling his arm across my shoulders to support his weight. The poor sod stumbled but stayed vertical, God love him. We had to move fast, get lost in the dense trees.

"Ready?" I asked. At Thomas's grunt, I propelled us forward, half-carrying, half-dragging his sorry arse away from the ambush site. Bullets whizzed past, kissing the trees as we fled. I fired blindly behind us with my free hand, not aiming for accuracy, just trying to make them think twice about following us into the woods.

We crashed through the underbrush, branches whipping against us. My lungs burned with effort, struggling to keep Thomas on his feet as we scrambled up a steep incline that felt like it was designed by someone who really fucking hated people walking on flat land. His steps grew heavier, shoulders slumping. I gripped him tighter.

"Stay with me, Thomas," I urged. "Just a little farther."

Suddenly, a small figure darted out from the underbrush ahead. I raised my pistol, ready to fire, when the boy threw up his hands.

"Wait, it's me!" he squeaked. I lowered the gun with a sigh that could've deflated a bloody zeppelin.

"Jacob, what the actual shit are you doing here?" I demanded.

The scrawny kid ran up beside me, ducking as another shot whizzed by. "I saw you were in trouble so I followed," he said, as if that was the most sensible decision since sliced bread.

"Of course you bloody did," I scoffed. The kid was about as stealthy as a brass band in a library, but his timing was impeccable. "Grab his other arm," I commanded.

Together, we hauled a fading Thomas through the trees while bullets nipped at our heels like angry hornets. I fired another shot behind us, the sharp retort buying a precious few seconds.

Up ahead, I spied the carriage waiting on the road. Renewing my grip on Thomas's arm, I poured every ounce of strength into a final burst of speed. We crashed through the last stand of trees and I all but threw Thomas onto the carriage bench.

"Go!" I yelled at Jacob as I scrambled up beside Thomas. The horses lurched into motion before I even had the door closed, hooves pounding down the road. I risked a glance behind us to see our pursuers emerge from the woods, shouting in frustration as we escaped.

I sank back against the seat, chest heaving more from adrenaline than exertion. Damn corset. Next to me, Thomas moaned through gritted teeth, his face alarmingly pale, blood oozing through his fingers like a particularly gruesome fountain. A cold claw of fear grabbed my heart. This wasn't how things were supposed to happen.

When we arrived at Thomas's townhouse, I sent Jacob running to fetch the doctor like his arse was on fire. My head spun with wild thoughts as I helped Thomas inside, easing him onto the settee. He grimaced, sweat beading on his brow.

Kneeling beside him, I gingerly peeled back his fingers to examine the wound. The hole oozed blood at an alarming rate. I grabbed a cloth and pressed down hard to try and slow it. Thomas groaned, his body going rigid.

"Just hold on," I urged. "We're getting you a doctor." Inside, doubts nagged at me. Thomas's face had gone gray, his breaths shallow. I could almost hear the sands of time slipping away as his lifeblood stained the settee crimson.

This was all my fault. If I hadn't involved Thomas, he would be safe right now, tucked away with his books and artifacts. Not bleeding out on the settee from a gunshot meant for me. Acid guilt gnawed at my insides.

Thomas's eyes fluttered open, glassy with pain but still intensely blue. He mustered a grin that could've been charming if it weren't for the circumstances. "Quite the adventure you've gotten me into, Miss Templeton."

I shook my head, blinking back tears. "I never meant for this to happen. I'm so sorry."

With effort, he lifted a trembling hand to my cheek. "You have nothing to apologize for. I chose this fight. For you. For Amelia." His voice cracked. "Don't give up now."

His faith in me, even hovering at death's door, was a lump I couldn't swallow. I clutched his hand to my chest.

"I won't give up," I vowed. "I'll make that bastard Stanton pay if it's the last thing I do."

Thomas's eyes shone with pride before slipping closed again. He drifted into restless semi-consciousness, muttering deliriously. I kept pressure on the wound, silently begging time to stop its relentless march.

Finally, the door burst open and Jacob rushed in, the doctor on his heels carrying a large leather bag. The older man's forehead creased with concern as he took in the blood-soaked scene. He quickly washed his hands in a basin and opened his bag to reveal rows of gleaming instruments.

"I'll need space to work," he said gruffly. "Go wait outside."

I started to protest but the doctor silenced me with a stern look. This was not a man to be trifled with. Reluctantly, I stepped into the night air, praying the doctor could achieve a miracle.

Alone on the doorstep, the day's events crashed down on me.

Leaning against the doorframe for support, I took deep breaths trying to slow my racing heart. The image of Thomas's ashen face, twisted in pain, seared into my mind. Once again, someone I cared for teetered on the brink of death because of me.

I gazed up at the inky sky in search of answers. The stars glittered coldly, indifferent to our plight. Somewhere out there, Stanton sat smugly plotting his next act of cruelty. He would keep destroying lives unless someone stopped him.

For years I'd tried to avoid this, retreating into my quiet life at the bookshop. But evil like Stanton's doesn't just fade away, not unless you snuff it out at the source. Which meant only one path forward: I had to take him down, whatever it took. For Amelia. For Thomas. For all the lives ruined by his wickedness.

This wasn't just about justice anymore. It was personal now. Stanton had crossed a line, and I was going to make him pay.

The door opened behind me, pulling me from vengeful thoughts. The doctor emerged, face unreadable. My throat went dry.

"Will he pull through?" I asked, heart thumping like a drum in my ears.

The doc gave a weary sigh, the weight of his years etched on his face. "I've done what I can. Stopped the bleeding and stitched him up. But the ball tore through his innards something awful." He shook his head. "It's in the hands of the Almighty now. Best to prepare yourself."

Chapter 16

The charcoal sketch was an exact likeness, every detail perfectly captured in harsh shadows and contours. The imposing edifice of Stanton's office building loomed blocks ahead, a hulking monstrosity of Gothic stone and iron. Six towering stories of polished rock and darkened windows, not a light burning at this late hour. Except for one. The top floor.

I studied the drawing intently, tracing the path my fingertips would soon follow up its unforgiving facade. No handholds, barely any grooves to grasp. It would be slow going, with every inch up that unforgiving wall a battle between me, gravity, and the distinct possibility of an abrupt introduction to the cobblestones.

I folded the sketch carefully and tucked it into the inner pocket of my cloak. The heavy wool enveloped me in musty darkness, perfect for tonight's work. I flipped the hood up, cinched it tight, and headed for the building.

The frigid caress of the night breeze raised goosebumps on the small bits of skin that were still exposed. I melded with the shadows, just another patch of darkness in a city that had cornered the market on gloom. My breath emerged in damp clouds, scattering like phantoms in my wake. The only sounds were the rasp of my boots on cobblestones and the shiver of bare branches overhead.

The more respectable bits of London fell away, leaving the stark, sleeping shapes of warehouses and closed-up shops. I slipped through the constricting passageways, the scaffolding of commerce looming above me. This part of the city belonged to the night - deserted, isolated, the perfect playground for my mischief.

As I walked, I allowed myself to think of Amelia with her knowing green eyes that had seen too much. She reminded me so much of another girl, from another life, whose flame had been snuffed out far too soon by men like Stanton. I would not, could not fail again.

And Thomas. Reckless, maddening Thomas who was fighting for his life because of me. I shook all thoughts from my head and kept moving.

The alley opened up before me, a broad avenue glistening under the muted moonlight. My destination stood at the far end, a hulking shadow backlit by the night sky. As I walked, I stared at the building that represented everything I despised, entitlement, greed, cruelty for its own sake.

With a pace that could've outrun a scandal, I closed the distance. As I approached, the edifice expanded above me, blotting out the sky, the top disappearing into darkness. Up close, the stone and iron took on an imposing solidity, like a great beast curled up to sleep. But I knew its secrets. I knew its weaknesses.

I slipped in between the neighboring structure that leaned close to create a tight, passageway. Cobwebs stirred as I slid past, dust and the skittering of creatures unknown cascading around me.

At the back corner, I found what I was looking for - a maintenance ladder leading up into the belly of the beast. Iron rungs were bolted precariously into the stone, disappearing upwards.

I grasped the bottom rungs and began my ascent, the cold of the metal biting into my palms even through my gloves. I climbed methodically, steadily, each movement controlled and precise. The physical exertion steadied my racing heart, forced my circling thoughts into stillness. There was only the next rung, the next inch higher.

The sounds of London faded below me as I rose. The only noise was the rush of wind in my ears and the rasp of my breath.

As my body warmed to the exertion, the cold night air began to sink its teeth into any exposed skin. I suppressed a shiver, glad for the encompassing cloak.

I was halfway up the featureless wall when my foot slipped on a patch of icy metal. For a heart-stopping second, I was in free fall, my stomach performing a sickening lurch. But my grip held firm, the jolt wrenching my shoulders violently. I hung still, eyes squeezed shut, willing my racing heart to slow. Don't look down, I told myself firmly. Keep moving.

Hand over hand, lungs burning, I continued upward. My world narrowed to an endless repetition of strain and release, cold metal and colder stone. I moved in a trance, my thoughts curled deep inside, hoarding my energy. Every part of me shook, down to each single cell as I forced my mind to forget its fear.

A flicker of light from a lower window made me freeze. I pressed myself flat against the frigid stone, praying the shadows concealed me. The light died, and I chewed myself out in whispers. "Don't cock it up now, Lizzy." I needed to be more careful or everything I had sacrificed would be for nothing.

I willed warmth into my stiff fingers and resumed the ascent, ignoring the ache of my overexerted muscles. Almost there. Amelia's face shone encouragingly in my mind's eye. And Thomas, a silent guardian watching over me. I pushed myself harder.

Vertigo tried to waltz with me then, a most unwelcome suitor, as the ground swirled below. Frantically I squeezed my eyes shut, clinging like a limpet to the side of the building, my forehead pressed hard against the ladder. Breathe, just breathe.

I forced my eyes open, made myself look up into the night sky and take deep, steadying breaths. The paralyzing fear receded slightly, and I began to climb again, my legs leaden and clumsy.

There. Just below the roofline crouched my prize - an arched window, Stanton's office. The ledge beneath was barely wide enough to perch on, but it was my sliver of hope and my ticket in.

Dangling a good fifty feet above London's most unforgiving

cobblestones, my fear of heights was showing itself to be a right drama queen, hogging the spotlight without a shred of shame.

A frigid gust of wind buffeted me as I clung to that rickety ladder for dear life, cursing under my breath. My fingers were numb with cold by the time I managed to haul myself up to Stanton's office window.

I fumbled in my pocket for the heavy rock I'd brought along. It wasn't exactly advanced spy gear, but a good old-fashioned manual smash seemed like the best way to grab this asshat's attention.

I reared back and hurled the rock with all my might.

The glass exploded with a magnificent crash, shattering the silence.

As I shakily climbed through, careful, even though I'd worn my thickest leather gloves, I found myself face-to-face with the devil himself, Lord Stanton. After all this time, after endless nights spent poring over maps and documents, after risky infiltrations and secret meetings in seedy taverns, I had finally reached the viper's nest.

Stanton's beady eyes glinted in the low candlelight as he regarded me with amusement. "Well, well," he purred, "if it isn't the elusive Elizabeth Templeton. To what do I owe this unexpected pleasure?"

I fought to keep my expression neutral. "Surely you know why I'm here, Stanton."

He clasped his hands behind his back and began to slowly circle me, like a shark preparing to strike. "I confess, your motives are not entirely clear to me. Perhaps you'd care to...enlighten me?"

My fingers itched for the knife concealed in my waistband, but I restrained myself. I had to keep him talking long enough to get the information I needed.

"Cut the bullshit, Stanton. I know all about your little enterprise - the bribes, the blackmail, the disappearances. It ends tonight."

Stanton paused in his circling to study me with renewed

interest. "Is that so? And you presume to stop me all by yourself?" He chuckled. "My dear, you have no idea what you're up against."

"I know enough," I said coldly. "Your days of exploiting the innocent are over. Now where is Amelia Thompson?"

At the mention of Amelia's name, Stanton's lips curled into a cruel smile. "Ah yes, the pretty young peasant girl. I believe I've...misplaced her."

My blood boiled at his flippant tone, but I kept my voice low and steady. "If you've harmed one hair on her head, I swear to God-"

"You'll what?" Stanton cut me off. "Kill me? Turn me over to the authorities? Please." He waved a dismissive hand. "I own the authorities in this city."

He was right about that. Stanton's network of bribes and extortion had infiltrated every level of law enforcement. He was virtually untouchable through proper legal channels. But I wasn't about to admit it.

"Where is she?" I repeated through gritted teeth.

Stanton smiled patronizingly. "Now, now, before we discuss business, why don't you take a seat? Have some tea?"

Before I could react, he grabbed my arm in an iron grip and forced me down into a velvet upholstered chair. I tensed, ready to fight, but he'd already turned away to pour tea from an ornate silver pot as if we were two biddies at a garden party. The casual violence of the gesture set my nerves on edge. Stanton was accustomed to taking exactly what he wanted, without consequence. I had to shake that unflappable confidence of his.

When he handed me the delicate teacup, the genteel facade disappeared from his eyes. "Drink," he commanded.

I merely arched an eyebrow at him and set the cup aside. We both knew I wouldn't leave here without learning Amelia's location, one way or another.

Stanton settled into the chair opposite me, observing me closely, then waved his hand flippantly. "Miss Thompson's situation is...unfortunate. But girls like her are the cost of business," he shrugged, like he was discussing the weather.

I leaned in, all the fury of Hell in my eyes. "She's an innocent young woman who lost her family, not a pawn for you to exploit."

"Innocent?" Stanton scoffed. "No one in this city is innocent, my dear. Surely your...background gave you that perspective."

I bristled. "My past is none of your concern. And if you're quite done attempting to distract me, perhaps we could return to the matter of Amelia's whereabouts."

Stanton slowly swirled the tea in his cup. "You seem rather invested in the fate of that girl. Tell me...why is that?"

When I didn't answer, he continued, "Could it be you see yourself in her situation? An orphan with nowhere to turn, no one who cares if you live or die?"

I fought to keep my breathing even. He was trying to get under my skin, throw me off balance. I couldn't let him succeed.

I bristled. "Let's stick to the topic, shall we? Amelia. Where is she?"

Setting down his cup, Stanton steepled his fingers and regarded me with a calculating expression. "I'll make you a deal. Come work for me, and I'll tell you where Miss Thompson is. With your particular skill set, you'd be a valuable asset to my operation."

I couldn't help it, I laughed. It burst out of me like a cork from a champagne bottle—only less celebratory and more 'what the fuck?' Stanton and friggin' Caldwell must have had a bloody discussion about me. "You must be joking. I would never lower myself to serve the likes of you."

Stanton's eyes flashed with menace, but his tone remained calm. " I am dead serious, Elizabeth. Together we could accomplish great things."

He rose and came to stand uncomfortably close behind my chair. I tensed, ready to strike if need be.

"I saw the way you took out my men," he murmured. "Quick, efficient, no hesitation. You enjoyed it, didn't you?"

I stared straight ahead, refusing to acknowledge his words.

He placed his hands on my shoulders in a falsely familiar gesture. "You try to hide it, try to deny your true nature, but I know what you really are. We're alike, you and I."

In one swift movement, I twisted from his grasp and drew my dagger, pressing the tip right over his heart. "We are nothing alike," I growled. "Now tell me where she is before I paint this rug with your blood."

Stanton glanced down at the dagger impassively. "Kill me and you'll never find her."

Fuck. Maintaining the knife's position as rage boiled inside me, it took every ounce of my self-control not to drive the dagger straight into Stanton's black heart. But I couldn't risk it, not while Amelia's life still hung in the balance.

I'm going to give you one chance, Stanton. Release Amelia and drop all claims to her, or I'll make sure your next drink is a pint of the Styx."

Stanton arched an eyebrow. "Come now Elizabeth, let's be civil. I'm sure we can reach an arrangement that suits us both."

I stepped forward until my face was inches from his. "The time for arrangements is over. Release her now or sign your own death warrant."

For a long moment Stanton just studied me in silence, his dark eyes boring into mine. I could almost see the calculations running behind them.

"I believe we've found ourselves at a bit of an impasse, Miss Templeton," Stanton croaked, Adam's apple bobbing.

"Seems that way," I replied calmly, giving the knife a little nudge to remind Stanton who had the upper hand here. Literally. "Although I'd say this situation favors me considerably more than you."

Stanton let out a nervous chuckle that ended in more of a whimper. "Yes, well, I suppose threatening a peer of the realm in his own office does grant you a modicum of leverage."

"You know, I wasn't always keen on threats and violence," I mused, shifting my weight slowly from one foot to the other to keep my muscles loose. "I used to think I could change the world with nothing but my wits and my words. How delightfully naïve I was back then."

I leaned in, my voice dropping to a conspiratorial whisper. "Then pricks like you showed me the ropes. Sometimes, to get justice, you need to grab life by the bollocks and twist."

The knife kissed his chest, and a bead of blood bloomed like a rose on his shirt.

"Now let's not do anything rash," he said, his breath quickening.

"Rash?" I cut him off with a harsh laugh. "You don't know the meaning of rash, old man. Ruthless, manipulative, sadistic - those words suit you better. Did you think I wouldn't put the pieces together? The missing girls. The bribes and backroom deals. The bone-chilling rumors whispered by your tenants and staff."

I leaned in until my nose nearly touched his. "You've woven quite the sordid web. Extortion. Assault. Kidnapping." I paused, regarding him with icy contempt. "You're the embodiment of everything foul and corrupt in this city. And your reckoning is long overdue."

"Ah, but do you know what all of that gets me? Anything and everything I want. And you could have the same. Follow your colleague and join me. I can give you anything your heart desires."

"You think I would stoop to Caldwell's level?" I scoffed. "The only agreement here is that you pay for your crimes. All the lives you've destroyed, all the pain you've caused. It ends tonight."

"You don't understand," he said. "I was only doing what was necessary to survive, same as anyone."

I let out a harsh laugh. "Survive? Is that what you call preying on innocent women?" My mind flashed to Amelia's face, so young and full of life. "You're the worst kind of monster."

I could see the exact moment Stanton decided to switch tactics. His eyes hardened even as his voice took on a patronizing tone.

"We're more alike than you care to admit, you and I. We both do what needs to be done to get what we want." His lips curled into a smile. "Go on, kill me. But then you'd be no better than the man you hate so much."

Oh, he was clever, this one. But I wasn't some fresh-faced ingénue he could manipulate. "Nice try. But we're nothing alike." I pressed the blade harder, my voice razor sharp. "I kill to protect. You kill for power. And that ends now."

I tensed, ready to drag the knife across his throat and end this once and for all. This was it. My moment of triumph. But...

Stanton seemed to sense my hesitation. "You need me alive. I'm the only one who knows where your precious Amelia is, after all."

The asshole was right, damn it. I needed to find Amelia, make sure Caldwell hadn't already...no, I couldn't think it. I was so close to taking Stanton down once and for all. But what if I was sacrificing Amelia in the process?

Stanton watched my internal struggle play out on my face. "Here's how this is going to go," he said calmly. " You need me breathing, Lizzy dear. And in return, I'll tell you exactly where to find Amelia Thompson."

Red hot rage flooded my veins. How dare he try to control me, use Amelia against me? I wanted to slash that smug look right off his face. But the thought of Amelia in danger tempered my fury. As much as I hated it, I needed Stanton. For now.

With immense effort, I lowered the knife. Relief washed over Stanton's face. He straightened his coat, regaining that infuriating air of superiority I longed to beat out of him.

"Excellent decision, Elizabeth," he purred. "I knew you would see reason."

"Spare me your theatrics," I snapped. "Where is she?"

Stanton rifled through his pockets until he produced a small piece of paper. He scribbled something down before holding it out to me. I wanted to lunge, grab him by the throat and shake the information out of him. But I controlled myself, taking the paper with a smile so tight it could strangle.

"This had better be accurate." My voice was ice. "Because if I find you've lied to me, there won't be a place in London you can hide. I will hunt you down and gut you like a fish. Are we clear?"

Genuine fear flashed across Stanton's face. He swallowed and gave a quick nod. Message received.

Without another word, I turned on my heel and strode away, clutching the piece of paper in my hand. I had what I needed. Now to find Amelia.

But as I stepped out into the night air, I felt no sense of victory. Only a bone-deep fury that Stanton had slipped through my grasp once again. Laughing at my inability to do what needed to be done. It gnawed at me, as relentless as the cold London rain piercing my skin. I'd thought to just go ahead and kill him anyway, but a tiny niggle wouldn't leave me be. What if he was lying?

Chapter 17

The address scribbled on the tattered paper clutched in my hand led me to the seediest part of town. I stood across the muddy street, hidden partly in shadow, as I observed the so-called "gentlemen's club" that was my destination. Even from the outside, it was clear this place was no simple tavern or club - it was a brothel, and an elite one at that, if the finery adorning the patrons stumbling drunkenly through the doors was any indication.

My guts twisted as I thought of Amelia being forced into this life of exploitation. I had to get her out, but even as determination coursed through me, an icy dread trickled down my spine. I'd seen places like this before, flesh markets where innocent girls were trapped in gilded cages of silk and shame. I knew the reality of what went on behind the velvet curtains and saccharine perfumes. Pretty wrappings hid dark secrets.

Drawing a breath, I steeled myself. I hadn't come this far just to walk away. For Amelia's sake, I had to try. But even as I psyched myself up for a fight, doubts nagged at me.

Two armed guards stood at the front entrance, conspicuously brandishing rifles - not the usual decor for even a high-class whorehouse. Their stance was alert, almost military. My senses screamed that those guards weren't meant to keep people out, they were there to keep the girls in.

This was no simple brothel. It was a prison.

Every instinct urged me to storm the place and get Amelia out. But if I barged in solo, I'd be hopelessly outgunned. I was good—damn good—but I couldn't take on Stanton's private army alone. And even if I succeeded in rescuing Amelia, what about the other girls imprisoned there? The cold truth was that if I didn't take down Stanton's entire vile operation, Amelia would simply be replaced within a week.

I needed help. Powerful help. But with Thomas hovering on death's door after our last brush with Stanton's goons, I had no one to turn to.

Frustration and despair bubbled up in me as I stared at those guarded doors, so close yet impossibly out of reach. I wanted to scream. To fight. To tear through any barrier between me and that poor girl who deserved so much better than this.

I slowly backed away, my heart fracturing with every step. I sent a silent promise into the night that I would come back for her. For all of them. Stanton would pay for his sins if it was the last thing I did.

Back at the bookshop, I couldn't stop replaying the image of those armed guards in my mind. Something about this reeked of being personal, as if Stanton had placed them there deliberately to torment me. He knew I would come for the girl. The message was clear - Amelia was beyond my reach. Just another prize locked away in Stanton's gilded cage. He was toying with me yet again.

I scrubbed a hand over my face, emotions churning. Goddammit, I needed a drink. And someone to talk to who wasn't comatose. God Thomas, I thought as I flopped onto a stool.

As if on cue, Jacob sauntered into the shop, his usual impish grin dimming when he saw my expression.

"Rough day, Miss Elizabeth?"

Despite myself, my lips quirked. "You could say that."

He already knew most of what was going on, so I figured it wouldn't hurt to unburden myself as I filled him in on the situation. He perched on the edge of my desk, brow furrowed. For a street kid, Jacob had a good head on his shoulders. Maybe he could see something I couldn't.

Before I could spill my guts, Oliver bumbled in. "Evening,

all!" he boomed, sending a cascade of books to the floor like autumn leaves.

The man had the delicacy of a hippopotamus in a glass factory, but he was trustworthy, and right now, I needed all hands on deck, even if one of those hands was more accustomed to holding a quill than a sword.

"We've got a situation, gents." I quickly recapped the day's events. "I'm open to ideas here, because I'm coming up empty."

"Good lord, how dreadful!" Oliver's hand went to his chest like a maiden aunt who's heard a swear word.

"No kidding." I dropped my head in my hands. "I can't just leave her, or any of those other girls there."

Jacob, with the earnestness of a pup wanting to please, suggested we find a way to make Stanton an offer he couldn't refuse. "Leverage."

I peered up at him. "Okay, well, people like Stanton, they care about power and money, right? So what if..." My brain whirred as a spark an idea began to take shape. I turned to Oliver. "Ever dabbled in the art of forgery, Ollie?"

He blinked. "Well, I've never actually tried, but I suppose I could attempt—"

"Great. Grab some parchment." I cracked my knuckles. This batshit crazy plan just might do the trick.

And just like that, we were cooking up a scheme that was either the work of pure, unadulterated genius or the kind of madness that gets you a one-way ticket to Bedlam.

An hour later, the forged document was complete. It was a piece of bloody art…if I hadn't known better, even I would have believed it was written in Stanton's own hand.

I met Jacob's gaze. "You sure you're okay delivering this solo?"

He scoffed. "I know every inch of this city. I'll slip in and out, easy as pie."

"Here." I slid a few coins into his palm. "Payment for services rendered. And be careful, yeah?"

Jacob pocketed the coins and tipped an imaginary hat. "Aren't I always?"

Off he went, melting into the night like a shadow with a secret, as I sent a prayer to any higher power bothering to listen that this ridiculous ruse would work. Then Oliver and I turned our attention to phase two.

We bent over the floorplan like two conspirators plotting to steal the crown jewels – except our jewel was a dusty, forgotten warehouse on the arse-end of town.

I cracked my knuckles, mind spinning with ideas. Stanton thought he was so damn clever with his little power plays and head games. We'd see who was clever now. No one hurt my friends and got away with it.

But I couldn't stop worrying about Jacob. I paced the shop, unable to focus on anything as I waited for him to return. A thousand horrific scenarios ran through my mind. What if Caldwell's men caught him planting the forged document? What if they didn't buy it and realized it was a set-up? Jacob was resourceful, but he was still just a kid. If anything happened to him because of me...

The door creaked open and I whirled around. Jacob strolled in, whistling, with not a hair out of place.

I sagged in relief. "Thank god. Did it work?"

"Slipped it right under their noses. Caldwell's man nearly choked on his ale when he saw it." Jacob laughed. "Should've seen his face. Looked fit to piss himself."

Despite the circumstances, I barked out a laugh. "Brilliant. Hopefully that lights a fire under Stanton's ass." I reached out to squeeze the kid's shoulder. "Seriously, Jacob. Thank you. I know it wasn't easy."

He ducked his head, cheeks flushing. "Aw, weren't nothing. Happy to help."

"Right." I straightened. "Now for phase two. Time to royally piss off Caldwell."

Jacob's grin turned wicked. "This I gotta see."

Over the next two days, Jacob worked his street kid magic to spread rumors that Caldwell had taken over an abandoned warehouse and staffed it with armed guards running illicit operations. His informants were damn effective—soon the gossip spread through both the seedy underworld and the upper crust elites.

Meanwhile, Oliver and I rigged up enough boobytraps and tripwires in that warehouse to make a special operations spy team proud. The dim lighting of the abandoned warehouse cast long shadows across the dusty concrete floor. My eyes swept over the empty space, scanning for any signs of trouble as my fingers deftly secured the nearly invisible tripwire at about shin height. I had to hand it to Oliver—for all his bumbling ways, the man knew his stuff when it came to rigging up some devious traps. Between the two of us, we'd managed to turn this place into a real house of horrors…one giant mousetrap just waiting to snap shut on Caldwell and Stanton.

I finished tying off the last wire and crept silently through the maze of shelving units and old machinery left to rot decades ago. My soft-soled boots didn't make a sound as I moved, my senses tuned to any shift in my surroundings. Adrenaline hummed through my veins but my breathing remained steady.

Time to move into position. I scaled a sturdy looking shelving unit, using the crossbeams like a ladder until I'd reached a height that provided a decent vantage point while still keeping me concealed in shadow. My dark clothes helped me blend right in to the gloom. For all the flattering traits of a good gown, today was a day for pants.

Now to wait, like a predator anticipating the arrival of its prey.

Still, knowing what needed to be done and actually doing it were two very different beasts. The familiar demons of doubt and guilt threatened to rise up and swallow me whole if I let them. I'd been down this road enough times to know how easily good intentions could be twisted down into darkness. How many times had I told myself the end would justify the means, only to watch everything crumble into ash?

No. I shoved the doubts aside forcefully, clenching my jaw until my teeth ached from the pressure. The past was written in stone. Nothing I could do would change it now. But the future —the future was still unformed clay, ready to be molded by the hands of the present. My hands.

This was about protecting people who couldn't protect themselves. People like Amelia who'd refused to let Stanton extinguish her inner light, no matter how cruelly he tried. She deserved a life free from fear and pain. From men like Stanton who fancied themselves gods and held no regard for those they trampled underfoot in their lust for control and power.

My hands curled into fists as rage simmered in my blood. Stanton would never lay a hand on her or anyone else ever again after tonight. I swore it.

The distant rumble of an engine outside the warehouse pulled me from my darkening thoughts. I tensed, every muscle coiled tight as a spring. The next few minutes would determine everything. If Caldwell detected even a hint of something amiss, she would disappear back into the shadows before Stanton arrived. All of this would be for nothing.

I forced myself to take slow, deep breaths, listening as the car approached. The engine cut off, followed by the opening and closing of doors. Multiple sets of footsteps crunched across grit and gravel, growing louder as they drew near. I counted four distinct cadences—Caldwell walked with a confident, unhurried stride. The others were her muscle, herding closely around her. Four targets, unaware they were about to walk straight into a carefully laid trap.

The warehouse door creaked open on rusty hinges, then clanged shut. I watched from my perch through gaps in the shelving as Caldwell strolled inside, her three associates fanning out around her, hands hovering at their holsters. Her keen gaze swept the space, likely cataloguing every detail. She wouldn't have gotten as far as she had in this world by being careless.

I remained utterly still, barely daring to breathe. The shadows cloaked me well, but it only took one misstep to give myself away. Caldwell finished her inspection and nodded for her men to scout ahead. As they moved forward, I caught a hint of tension in her posture. The cock of her head, the tightness around her eyes—she anticipated an ambush even if she couldn't yet detect one. No doubt her instincts had kept her alive this long. I would have to trust that her newfound suspicion of Stanton would override her usual caution.

At least I didn't have to wait long. No more than five minutes after Caldwell's arrival, I picked up the distant slam of another car door. Stanton, right on time. He certainly couldn't be accused of lacking dramatic flair. The man seemed to relish his reputation—it struck fear into the hearts of his enemies and kept his followers fanatically loyal. I had to admit, the power trip probably felt damn good. At least until it came crashing down around you.

Heavy footsteps signaled Stanton's approach. He entered with half a dozen of his lackeys. Perfect, having his men here meant a skeleton crew at best back at the brothel. His sneer of disdain upon seeing Caldwell said he considered her little more than a gnat to be crushed under his boot. Fool. She was exactly the kind of person to plunge a stiletto between his ribs when he least expected it.

"What a surprise to find you here," Stanton drawled as he swaggered further inside. The warehouse door slammed shut behind him with an ominous clang that carried the finality of a coffin lid. "I don't recall requesting the pleasure of your company this evening."

Caldwell's smile didn't reach her icy eyes. "And I don't recall needing your permission to do as I please."

"As brazen as ever." Stanton tsked under his breath. "When will you learn to mind your betters?"

"My betters?" Caldwell let out a sharp bark of laughter. "The only thing superior about you, darling, is your boundless arrogance. Though I suppose I should thank you for providing me with so many opportunities these past few months. Your incompetence has been rather profitable for me."

Stanton's expression darkened, all pretenses slipping away to reveal something far uglier beneath the surface. "Do not test me, woman," he snarled through clenched teeth. "You are forgetting your place."

"Oh, I know exactly where I stand." Caldwell took a bold step forward, cold fury emanating from every rigid line of her body. "Far above you and your crumbling empire built on manipulation and fear. But nothing lasts forever, does it?" Her red lips curved in a cruel, knowing smile. "Not even the great Lord Stanton."

I could almost see the sparks flying between them, two massive egos confined in one small space. They circled each other like rival lions, poised on the brink of violence. I tensed, ready to spring the trap.

"You honestly believe you can take me down?" Stanton scoffed. "You have no idea who you are dealing with."

"Nor do you," Caldwell shot back. "But your reign ends tonight. One way or another." Her hand drifted toward her hip.

Now. I yanked the first rope to disarm the tripwire, moving through the series quickly, closing up the main exits first to prevent escape. As the doors slammed down into place with an echoing boom, I triggered the release of half a dozen nets. They dropped from anchoring points high above, the weights at the edges giving them enough momentum to sail down over both Caldwell's and Stanton's heads. I didn't wait to watch the satisfying image of my enemies flailing and cursing as they were caught—I was already dropping to the ground and sprinting for better cover.

Chaos erupted through the warehouse. Stanton's roar of fury was drowned out by the click of guns being drawn and the crash of storage crates being overturned as Caldwell's men tried to take up defensive positions. I darted down an aisle, pressed my back against a shelving unit, and drew my own weapon. The familiar weight grounded me despite the adrenaline burning through my system like wildfire.

Deep breath. Wait for an opening. I had the element of surprise on my side—neither Caldwell nor Stanton had expected me to be waiting for them when they arrived. But I couldn't allow myself to get cocky. Properly cornered, even rats would turn savage when threatened.

The distant sound of police sirens wailed through the chilly night air, thanks, no doubt to a cleverly timed anonymous call on the part of my allies.

My gaze swept over the shadowy forms of Caldwell, Stanton, and their lackeys, all oblivious to my presence thanks to their heated argument, though they must have been very curious how they'd found themselves trapped. I allowed myself a grim smile. The final moves of this deadly game were about to play out, and for once, I held the upper hand.

The past few weeks had been a rollercoaster ride straight into the depths of the criminal underworld. Now here I stood, on the cusp of finally bringing down the vile Stanton and Caldwell. Getting both of them meant freedom for all the people they were blackmailing. All the people they'd paid off would have no choice but to follow the letter of the law, the scrutiny would be so intense.

My mind raced, calculating my next moves with the strategic focus honed over years of practice. One shot at glory, and I wasn't about to fuck it up.

My thoughts flashed briefly to Jacob and Oliver. I hoped the final errand I'd sent them on—to gather anyone and everyone they trusted and rescue Amelia and the others from Caldwell's clutches—was proceeding without trouble.

The argument between Caldwell and Stanton was beginning to rise to a fever pitch as they disentangled themselves from the nets. I silently edged backward, using their inattention and the shadowy clutter of the warehouse to disguise my movements. Though experience had taught me to avoid direct involvement where possible, I couldn't resist subtly influencing the conflict at hand.

"This deal we had...it's over, you backstabbing worm!" Caldwell spat, venom dripping from her elegantly accented voice. Though nearing sixty, she still cut an imposing figure, her silver coif and icy eyes radiating authority.

Stanton's weathered face creased into a scowl, his voice equally icy. "Need I remind you, your enterprise only thrives due to my generosity. Perhaps your memory fails you, Lady Caldwell."

I cleared my throat softly. Just enough for them to hear, if they were listening for it. Their heads swiveled toward the shadowy corner where I lurked. I held my breath, motionless.

Their eyes narrowed, but detecting nothing amiss, Caldwell retorted, "Generosity? Don't make me laugh, you pompous fool. I've lost count of all your double-crosses."

The atmosphere in the warehouse grew tense as their argument escalated. My plan had planted the seeds of suspicion perfectly. I slipped away, moving silently between the dusty stacks of crates and machinery. My dark clothing blended easily into the surroundings, the quarreling voices masking any slight noise.

I paused behind a corroded boiler, its bulky form providing temporary cover while I surveyed my path ahead. Caldwell's men stood armed and alert, their loyalty ensured through fear rather than respect. Stanton's entourage mirrored them, the warehouse now a standoff waiting to explode.

My opportunity came when Caldwell hissed, "I should have cut ties with you months ago. This city would be better off without your sniveling face."

Stanton's expression clouded with rage. "You'll regret those words, you pompous hag!" He reached for the revolver at his hip.

I didn't wait to see Caldwell's reaction. The moment Stanton's fingers curled around his weapon, I broke from my hiding spot, sprinting for the rear of the building. Not a second too soon - gunfire erupted, the warehouse descending into chaos.

My breath burned in my chest as I dodged and weaved

through the labyrinthine space. I flung myself behind a stack of crates just as a spray of bullets splintered the corner above my head. Wood fragments rained down as I gasped for air, the cacophony of shouts and gunfire deafening this close to the action.

"Find the girl!" a gruff voice bellowed over the din.

My cover had been blown.

No matter. I steadied my nerves with a slow exhale, then risked a glance around my makeshift barricade.

Three of Stanton's men prowled through the clutter, sweeping their lanterns in search of me. Light glinted off their firearms. I silently cursed my luck. Evading them in these close quarters would be tricky, though I had faced worse odds before. As long as I kept my wits about me, I could use their numbers against them.

I slipped through the shadows, moving perpendicular to their search pattern. They fanned out among the crates and machinery, focused on the open spaces. The first one went down over a trip wire with a glorious, high-pitched shriek. It took all I had in me not to giggle as I snuck into one of the narrow gaps that allowed me passage but which they overlooked in their haste.

One strayed too close and I struck, surging from the darkness to grab his gun arm. I wrenched it back savagely, using his weight as I slammed him face-first into a metal beam. He crumpled without a sound. I was gone before his unconscious body hit the floor, his lantern crashing down to cast monstrous shadows against the walls.

His companions whirled toward the noise, but I had already melted back into the maze of debris. Distance was key now. I sped through the warehouse, ducking low, my breathing tight and controlled. My senses strained for any hint of movement.

Up ahead I spotted it - a rusted staircase curling up into the rear corner of the warehouse. If I could reach its higher vantage point unseen, I could bide my time until the police arrived. I plotted my path, marking the pools of shadow and the locations of Stanton's remaining thugs.

I broke cover, sprinting for the stairs. Behind me, shouts rang out as they spotted my fleeing form. I took the steps two at a time, my hands clamped on the railing, refusing to look back. My legs burned from the effort but I was almost there.

The retort of gunfire spurred me higher. Bullets ricocheted off the heavy machinery around me, the shots wild in the dim lighting. I hauled myself onto the exposed walkway, scrambling up into the depths of the rafters. I'd be fully hidden now with the freedom to move around the entire space in shadow. Breathing hard, I peered at the scene below.

My pursuers milled in confusion, their quarry apparently vanished. I allowed myself a fierce grin. Let them scramble about down there, chasing their own tails. I was in control now.

Settling into a crouch, I crept along the beams, keeping to the shadows beneath the exposed roof. Outside, the wail of approaching sirens grew louder. The standoff below devolved into chaos as Caldwell and Stanton's forces realized the imminent arrival of the police, and no matter how many crooked cops they had in their pockets, there would be no getting around a giant raid. Not exactly how I would have chosen to handle them—they deserved far worse than a cushy jail stint—but the result was the same. Justice was at hand.

Some of Caldwell's men made a break for the side door, pulling furiously at the heavy wooden barricade, only to find once they broke through, it was blocked by a mass of uniforms storming the warehouse. In moments, the remaining criminals were surrounded, their bravado evaporating. The jig, as they say, was spectacularly up.

From my perch I watched officers slap handcuffs on Caldwell and Stanton. The self-satisfied smirks had finally been wiped from their faces. I allowed myself a moment of satisfaction at the scene. We had cut the head off this particular snake. Now the work could begin dismantling the rest of their rotten empire.

My moment of triumph proved short lived. The piercing beam of a policeman's lantern swung upward, blinding me for a split second before I could shrink back. Too late. A voice bellowed out, "There's someone hiding up there! You two, get up that staircase, now!"

"Buggeration," I whispered. So close, yet my luck had run out. Perhaps it was for the best. I could hardly have walked out the front door unnoticed regardless. Resigned, I moved to the stairwell and raised my hands, making my way down the exposed stairs as two officers ascended toward me.

Chapter 18

The cold metal of the chair bit through my trousers as I sat in the dimly lit interrogation room. The lingering chill from the frigid night air had seeped into my bones, and the austere surroundings did little to warm me.

I'd been there for what felt like a geological era, with the same four walls for company and the occasional visit from detectives who seemed to have gotten their degrees in Bastardry from the University of Arsehole. They flung accusations mixed with snippets of information from my past, intended to trip me up. I met them with calm denials, giving away nothing. The truth was too unbelievable, even for men whose job it was to find it.

A melancholic sigh escaped my lips. I missed the simple comforts of my little bookshop, the rich scent of leather and parchment that welcomed me every morning. Oliver, always had a hot cup of tea ready for me, his chipper greeting a balm for my weary soul.

That all seemed a lifetime away now. Here in this cold, lifeless room, I had only my spinning thoughts and regrets for company, my mind retracing the tumultuous events that had landed me in this situation.

It was supposed to have been a new beginning. When I walked away from my old life as a spy years ago, I wanted nothing more than peace and stillness. The bookshop was my refuge, each day folding gently into the next without incident. I tended my little corner of the world contentedly, wanting no part of the danger and deceit that had once consumed my existence.

But the past, as it often does, had come back to haunt me, and when Amelia walked in that fateful night, I knew I had to act, to use my skills to uncover the truth. But that choice unlocked the floodgates, releasing a torrent of consequences beyond my control. And now there I was, stripped of my freedom, my future uncertain.

The door creaked open and harsh light flooded the dreary room, rousing me from my contemplations. I tensed, expecting another round of fruitless interrogation. But instead of the surly detectives who had been my only visitors, an unexpected and welcome face appeared.

"Thomas!" I gasped as he hobbled into the room, leaning heavily on a cane. Despite the late hour and his recent brush with death, Thomas's eyes shone bright with determination.

My shock at seeing him quickly turned to anger. "Just what do you think you're doing here? You should be at home resting, not gallivanting about the city."

A faint smile played about his lips. "Come now Elizabeth, you didn't really think I'd leave you here alone?"

His voice held a teasing lilt, but his jaw was set stubbornly. I knew that tone all too well. Thomas had a protective streak as wide as the Thames, and a matching tendency to throw himself headfirst into hazardous situations, especially if it meant saving someone he cared about. Which at the moment, seemed to be me.

As vexing as his recklessness could be, part of me thrilled at the evidence of his devotion. Thomas was unlike any other relationship I had known. Our connection had snuck up on me, like the first cautious shoots of spring after the endless winter. What had started as mutual intellectual curiosity had deepened into something rich, sensual, and delicate, still unfolding each day.

I softened my tone. "Thomas, I appreciate your dedication, misguided as it may be, but you mustn't risk your health, especially when I'm resigned to accept my fate."

"Ah, and that's where you're mistaken," Thomas replied.

"I didn't come here empty-handed." With a flourish, he reached into his satchel and retrieved a sheaf of papers. "I've been digging around Caldwell's townhouse. Her locked desk drawer yielded a number of interesting documents, including transaction records between herself and one Lord Stanton."

My mind raced. With this and the research he'd done into the money trail, Thomas had essentially gift-wrapped the detectives everything they needed to focus their investigation on Stanton and Caldwell, and in turn, take that focus off me.

Before I could express my overflowing gratitude, Thomas beckoned toward the doorway. A petite young woman stepped hesitantly into the room.

"Amelia!" I ran to the girl and flung my arms around her.

At that moment, as if summoned by providence, the door swung open and two detectives strode in.

"Here's the information I was telling you about," Thomas said, smoothly redirecting their attention to the evidence he had uncovered, laying out connections between Caldwell, Stanton, and signs of illegal activity. To her credit, Amelia gathered her courage and shared all that had happened to her, noting that it was all Stanton's doing.

I could see the gears turning in the detectives' minds as they processed the information. Thomas had handed them an irresistible trail to follow, laden with political intrigue and scandal. Their posture shifted from aggression to eager curiosity, as I realized with immense relief that they must not be on the man's payroll. Thank goodness for small mercies. And, you know, giant ones too. They temporarily set aside their suspicion of me as their focus zeroed in on this juicier target.

After what seemed an eternity of pointed questions, clarifications, and review of documentation, they finally conceded there was ample cause to redirect the investigation. I observed Thomas puff up slightly as they complimented his investigative prowess, and had to suppress an affectionate grin. The man did love having his intellect praised.

To my tremendous relief, they agreed I could be released, at least for the time being. There remained loose ends to tie up, but the cloud of accusation had lifted. As we left the station, the icy night air felt sweeter than the freshest country breeze. I breathed deep, savoring my freedom.

Our motley group paused under the glow of a streetlamp. Amelia was teetering on the edge of collapse, worn out from the night's theatrics, and who knows what else before that, but she'd kept her composure like a champ.

I pulled her off to the side for a bit of privacy, bracing myself for the conversation ahead. Saving her from Lord Stanton's clutches had been my singular focus these past few weeks, consuming my every thought and action. And now here we were, at the messy end where we had to sift through the debris.

I was struck by how young she looked, barely twenty if she was a day. Too young to have endured what she'd been through. A lump of guilt lodged itself firmly in my throat, imagining her terror and helplessness. If only I had uncovered Stanton's vile scheme sooner.

"I'm so sorry, Amelia," I managed to choke out, the words thick with the weight of it all. "I should have found you faster, before he..." I couldn't bring myself to finish the thought. Before he sold her to a brothel. Before he crushed her spirit and took away her choices. Before he destroyed her innocence in his twisted pursuits.

But Amelia took my hands in her own delicate grasp. "Don't you dare apologize, Elizabeth," she said, her voice a balm. "Without you, I'd still be in that hell."

I shook my head, tears stinging my eyes. "You went through hell because of me. If I had exposed Stanton sooner..."

"Stop," Amelia interrupted, giving my hands a squeeze. "The past is done. What matters now is that I'm free. You freed me, Elizabeth."

She lifted her chin and in her eyes, I saw the flicker of the old fire, the one that had made me stick my neck out for her in the first place.

"I won't pretend it wasn't awful," she continued, a shadow

passing over her face. "But it's over now," she went on resolutely. "You saved me from that place. I can move on and build a new life, one where I make my own choices, without fear. I've been in this city with no help for a long time. It wasn't the first time I'd had to do these things for money, but now that I'm free, at least it will be on my own terms."

I suppose I wasn't surprised, a young woman without a family had few choices, but I had hoped she'd been spared that life. Overcome with emotion, I pulled Amelia into a fierce embrace. She hugged me back just as tightly, her body shaking with silent sobs. All the fear, rage and sorrow we'd been holding in came pouring out in a healing flood.

I don't know how long we stood there, wrapped in each other's arms, comforting and taking comfort. But gradually our tears slowed, leaving us both strangely at peace.

Amelia pulled back first, wiping her eyes and giving me a tremulous smile. "Thank you, Elizabeth, for everything. I'll never forget what you did for me."

I shook my head, throat still too tight to speak. Eventually, I found my voice again.

"You're free now to choose your own path, Amelia. Whatever you desire for your future, I will support you." I gave her hands one last comforting squeeze before letting go.

Amelia's smile grew more steady and she drew herself up taller. The light was back in her eyes. Seeing that, I knew I had done right by her. There would be hard days to come, trauma that left its scars, but Amelia had reclaimed her power, her dignity, her light.

When we finally parted, Amelia enveloped me in one last warm hug.

"Thank you, my friend," she whispered. And in her voice, I heard hope reborn.

Thomas kindly offered to escort Amelia home safely. She nodded shyly in agreement. I told them I would make my own way and, truth be told, I needed to be with my thoughts to process all that had happened. I also needed space to strategize my next steps. This was not over, not by far. Uncovering this plot had cracked open a doorway to my past I had barricaded shut long ago. I could not in good conscience walk away now and let wicked forces continue to hold sway. But it would be risky, and sacrifices would have to be made.

Thomas studied me with those piercing eyes that seemed to bore into my soul. "Will you be alright Elizabeth? I fear the night's chill will be an unwelcome shock after the stifling heat of that interrogation room."

His words flowed with courtesy, but underneath I detected a current of concern, perhaps guessing at my swirling thoughts. I assured him I would be fine and urged him to get himself and Amelia safely home.

We parted ways reluctantly. As their forms receded into the night, I felt the heavy burden of responsibility settle upon my shoulders. Amelia's wide-eyed innocence was seared into my mind. She reminded me so much of who I used to be, before disappointment and betrayal had hardened my heart.

Chapter 19

The next evening, I sat at my desk, sipping a cup of tea and trying to focus on the open book in front of me. But my mind kept wandering back to the events of the last few weeks - the confrontation with Stanton, the gunshot meant for me that found Thomas instead, our desperate escape into the night, the trap set to capture Caldwell and Stanton once and for all.

A knock at the front door jolted me from my thoughts. I placed the cup down and hurried to answer it, bracing myself for whoever was on the other side. I swung the heavy oak door open to find Thomas standing there looking mostly alert and steady on his feet.

"Thomas!" I exclaimed. "What on earth are you doing here? You should be resting."

He gave me a lopsided smile. "I could say the same for you. Thought I'd come by to check on the troublemaker."

I stepped back to let him in, closing the door behind us.

"Come on, let's get you sat down and taken care of," I said, leading him onto the living room.

Thomas eased himself into one of the plush leather chairs by the fireplace while I headed for the liquor cabinet.

"Are you sure with our injuries we should be imbibing in the hard stuff?" he called after me.

I dismissed his objection with a wave of my hand. "Medicinal purposes," I called back, drowning two tumblers in brandy as if it was holy water and we were exorcising demons.

I crossed back to the seating area and offered him one of the glasses. He accepted it with a resigned shake of his head, though I saw a hint of a smile playing on his lips. I settled into the chair opposite him, cradling my own glass.

For a few moments we sipped our drinks in silence. Despite the warm brandy sliding down my throat, I still felt a knot in my stomach. Thomas had risked his life for me, and I had almost gotten him killed.

"Listen..." I began hesitantly. "About what happened. I'm so sorry I put you in danger like that. It was careless and reckless of me to even consider confronting Stanton like that."

Thomas held up a hand. "Elizabeth, stop. You have nothing to apologize for. I chose that dance with danger just as much as you."

I looked down, unable to meet the sincerity in his gaze. "Maybe so, but it was still my fault. My foolish crusade against Stanton is not your burden to bear."

Thomas leaned forward intently. "On the contrary. That man has caused far too much harm in this city, harm that people like you and I need to put a stop to. Your fight is an honorable one."

I gave him a small smile, bolstered by his words yet still weighed down by guilt. We both took another sip of brandy before I spoke again.

I took a deep breath, steeling myself for the conversation ahead. Thomas and I had been dancing around each other for weeks now, our flirtation growing into something deeper. But if this was going to go any further, I owed it to him to come clean about certain parts of my past.

"Thomas, before this goes any further between us, there are some things you should know," I began, my voice about as steady as a three-legged table.

He frowned, looking concerned. "What is it, Elizabeth?"

I took a deep breath, feeling like I was tiptoeing across a tightrope. "In my business, it was encouraged to sometimes employ...unconventional methods. I don't shy away from using all the assets at my disposal to get the job done," I said carefully.

Thomas' eyes narrowed, but he simply nodded for me to continue.

"With certain men...men like Cassius, sometimes a more intimate encounter can loosen their tongues. I'm not ashamed to admit I've often used such means in the past when it helps me achieve my aims."

His expression was unreadable as a blank page so I barreled on.

"I've...given sexual favors to gain information. Allowed powerful men to feast on my body in exchange for secrets that aided the Crown."

I hesitated, the next part even harder to admit. "With Cassius, I provided a particularly enthusiastic finish to his massage to secure his secrets. And perhaps a little feast on my breast as well." The words were tumbling like an avalanche that couldn't be stopped. "I can't say I even hated it—often I've enjoyed it—and I will not apologize. A spy must use every asset at their disposal, after all. But still, I have carried guilt because of this thing between us, Thomas."

I finally raised my eyes to his, trying to gauge his reaction.

He exhaled deeply, meeting my watery gaze. After a few agonizing moments, he finally spoke. "It does not change the way I see you. You are a brilliant, determined woman. What you did, you did in service of a cause greater than yourself. I cannot fault you for that."

His words stunned me. I had expected anger, judgment, disgust at my confession. But instead, Thomas was responding with an empathy and understanding I did not deserve. I opened my mouth to express my immense gratitude, but no words came out. My heart felt too full.

"It is not my place to judge your past or your choices. You are beholden to no one. I know that our...association is still new. I cannot ask you to change who you are or how you live."

I reached across and placed my hand over his. "Thomas, this thing between us - it means the world to me. I don't want it to end because of my sordid history."

For the first time since I started my confession, Thomas gave me a real smile. He squeezed my hand gently. "Nor do I. Which is why I propose a different arrangement, one that suits both our independent natures."

I cocked my head curiously. Thomas straightened in his chair.

"We continue seeing one another, enjoying each other's company and passion. But without expectation or obligation. Our lives remain our own. You need not change your ways to appease me," he said, as casual as if he were discussing the weather, rather than suggesting we engage in horizontal congress at our leisure. He paused, looking at me meaningfully. "The heart wants what it wants. No one person can fulfill every need. I believe men and women should not be chained to just one partner."

I felt my eyes widen in surprise. Whatever I had expected Thomas to say, it certainly wasn't this.

"Well, my god, Thomas Callahan. Look at you being all modern and progressive," I said, giving him an appraising look. "I must say, I like your style."

He grinned. "Then you accept my proposal?"

I pretended to consider it for a moment. "Hmm, let me mull this over. A handsome, brilliant man wants to take me for abundant rolls in the hay with no rules or constraints? Um, where do I sign up?"

We both laughed, the mood between us shifting to something lighter, though still crackling with intimacy. I felt as if a weight had been lifted from my shoulders. Thomas knew my truth and accepted me still. It was more than I could have hoped for.

When the laughter subsided, Thomas slapped another topic on the table. "There is one more aspect to my proposal. Though unorthodox, I believe our partnership would be beneficial beyond the bedroom."

I raised an eyebrow, intrigued. "Go on."

"I propose we become collaborators of a kind. Combining your skills as an operative with my resources and connections. To do meaningful work, make this city a better place."

Now it was my turn to grip my glass tightly in surprise. Thomas wanted us to be crime fighting partners? It was the last thing I expected him to suggest.

"I thought you said you couldn't watch me kill myself," I reminded him.

Thomas tilted his head in agreement. "Indeed. But since then, I've learned that I was wrong. You, Elizabeth Templeton, are more capable than any person I've ever met. It would devastate me if anything happened to you, but I've come to realize that this is who you are. And, as they say, if you can't beat them, join them."

A smile quirked at my lips.

Thomas pressed on earnestly. "I've also come to realize that since this started, I've felt more alive than I have in years. Bringing justice to a lawless place like this, with someone like you by my side...it's the most thrilling prospect I can imagine."

The dregs of the brandy burned warm in my belly. My confession hung in the air between us, but instead of pushing him away, it seemed to draw him closer. The candlelight cast a soft glow across his rugged features, but his eyes were intense as they searched mine.

"Truly?" I asked. "Even knowing who I am and what I'm capable of?"

His lips formed into a sly half-smile that made my pulse flutter despite myself. "Especially because of who you are," he said. "I've never met a woman quite like you, Elizabeth Templeton. You fascinate me, challenge me...excite me."

His words sent a delicious shiver down my spine. I stood up to brush my lips teasingly against his.

"Well then," I purred, "I suppose I shall have to think about it, Mr. Callahan."

He made a low sound in his throat before capturing my mouth in a searing kiss. My hands threaded through his hair, and I leaned into him, until he let out the slightest whimper.

I pulled back. "Thomas, I'm so sorry. I forgot about your injuries."

The panic on my face must have been funny, since he let out a little chuckle.

"Don't worry, anything we do will be well worth the pain, I'm sure."

"No," I said, stepping away from him.

But then his lips turned into the most adorable pout and I found myself wanting to please him in ways he'd never forget.

"Sit back, I know just the thing," I said.

With a small smirk, he eased himself deeper into the chair.

As I gently removed his bloodied shirt, I could see the pain etched on his face. But he didn't flinch as my fingers traced the lines of his injuries. Instead, he looked at me with a mixture of gratitude and desire that made my heart race.

My hands lingered on his chest as I leaned in to kiss him. Our lips met softly at first, but the passion between us quickly intensified. We kissed deeply, our tongues dancing together as we explored each other's mouths.

As our kiss broke, I looked into Thomas's eyes and saw a hunger that matched my own. Without hesitation, I began to undo his trousers slowly, savoring every inch of his body as it was revealed to me. His skin was warm and smooth beneath my touch, and I could feel the tension in his muscles easing as I cared for him.

When I reached his erection, I paused for a moment to look at it with appreciation. It was hard and throbbing, a testament to the desire that still burned between us. Without another word, I bent down and took him into my mouth, worshiping at the altar of his manhood like a devoted acolyte. As I paid deliciously detailed homage, the look he gave me was pure sin, as he groaned in pleasure. His hands gripped my hair tightly, guiding my movements as I suckled him with an odd combination of gentleness and fervor that surprised even me. The taste of him was intoxicating, and I couldn't get enough.

As he neared his climax, his breathing grew heavier, and his hips bucked slightly against my face. I could feel the tension building within him, and I knew that it wouldn't be long before he exploded.

"Oh Christ Elizabeth, may I?" he asked, ever the gentleman.

I pulled away just long enough to pant, "yes, please," as—with a loud groan—Thomas thrust himself deep into my mouth, his sweetness pouring into me. I swallowed every drop eagerly, savoring the taste of him.

Moments later, as he slowly pulled out of my mouth, Thomas looked down at me with a mixture of surprise and admiration in his eyes. "You're something else," he whispered hoarsely. "I don't think I've ever felt anything like that before.

I smiled up at him, feeling a sense of pride swell within me. "I do aim to please," I replied flirtatiously.

"My god, yes, that was most pleasing," he said, head lolling to one side. "But now I seem to find myself utterly exhausted."

"Bed then, shall we?" I asked.

"On one condition," Thomas said. "Since I'm naked, I think you ought to be too."

The smirk hit my lips before I realized it, and I let out an exasperated breath. "Fine, if you insist," I said. "But no funny business. You're too hurt."

"As long as I can look at you, I'm a happy man."

I smiled and gave him a side eye, as I slowly began to unlace my dress.

The dawn's early light filtered through the curtains, casting a soft glow across Thomas's sleeping face. I propped myself up on one elbow, studying his features. The usual intensity was gone, replaced by an unexpected vulnerability. His salt and pepper stubble, the lines etched across his brow from years of deep thinking, the silver strands glinting amidst the dark—all details made more intriguing by the rare unguarded moment.

As he began to stir. I pressed a feather-light kiss to his temple.

"Rise and shine, sleeping beauty."

One blue eye cracked open, still bleary with sleep. "What bloody time is it?" His voice came out low and gravelly.

"Early. The day awaits, full of mystery and adventure."

He squinted at my cheerfulness. "How are you so disgustingly upbeat at this ungodly hour?"

"Years of training. I've been conditioned to function on minimal sleep." I gave him a cheeky grin.

"Speaking of years of training, about that whole partner proposition…"

I raised an eyebrow. "You want to discuss this now, while we're naked?"

He gave me a roguish wink. "No time like the present."

I rolled my eyes. "Fine. Make your case."

"You and I both have passions that drive us. Yours for justice"—his eyes held mine intently—"mine for uncovering mysteries. Together we're unstoppable. Think of how many people we could help."

"Or how much damage we could do," I added quietly. Images from my past flickered through my mind, broken bodies and blood-spattered streets. The ghosts lingered in the corners, murmuring regret.

He reached to me, gripping my hand. "You can't let fear rule you. Not when you have so much to offer."

I wanted to believe him. To believe I was more than the sum of my sins. But the ghosts whispered warnings, reminding me that hope was merely the first step on the road to disappointment.

Still, looking into Thomas's resolute face, I felt myself wavering. I took a deep breath. "Alright, partner. Where do we start?"

His eyes lit up. "Funny you should ask." He leaned back with a smug grin. "I took the liberty of getting us started. I've got a missing person that needs locating."

"A missing person's case?" I asked, skeptical.

"Not just any missing person. Lady Caroline, daughter of Duke Andrew Fairfax."

The name sounded vaguely familiar. "Fairfax…as in one of the most influential families in England?"

Thomas nodded. "The one and only. Lady Caroline disappeared without a trace three nights ago just blocks from the family's London estate. No ransom note, no clues, nothing."

I frowned. "Have the police been informed?"

"Of course. But you know as well as I do, they're useless with cases like these. Too many egos and agendas." He raised an eyebrow. "I thought we could do some independent investigating."

I sighed, leaning back. "So that's what this surprise partnership is about? Investigating a high society kidnapping?"

"Think of it as a test run. Our chance to see if we actually make good partners." He inclined his head. "So what do you say? Are you ready for an adventure, Elizabeth Templeton?"

His eyes gleamed with anticipation. I knew that look well—it was the same restless hunger that had led me down dangerous paths before. Only now, I had someone to walk those perilous roads with.

This was madness. Utter madness born of pure foolish hope. I should walk away before either of us got hurt.

Thomas watched me, patient and hopeful, a man of courage offering his steady hand to guide me from the darkness. How could I refuse?

"Well, partner, what are we waiting for? Adventure awaits." I grinned. "Let's go catch ourselves a kidnapper."

"Excellent," Thomas said, a grin stretched across his face. "There's just one thing we need to do first."

"Oh yeah? And what's that," I asked.

He smirked. "I was thinking a little sexual congress might help get our creative juices flowing."

"Thomas! You've just been shot. You can't be rollicking around in your condition…unless…you want me to go down on you again," I said, more than happy to oblige if that's what he was after.

"Oh no my dear, it's your turn," he said, pumping his eyebrows.

I opened my mouth to argue, but he put a hand up to stop

me. "There is still one part of my body that is in perfect working condition."

I tilted my head, confused.

"These babies," he said pointing to his lips. "Giddyap, darling," he said as he laid back down on the bed and shimmied his shoulders to settle in.

My heart started to race. "You are incorrigible," I said, though of course it didn't stop me from straddling him.

As I pressed my most sensitive area to those luscious, eager lips of his, I couldn't help but think that, in more ways than one, I was in for a hell of a wild ride.

Note From the Author

Thank you so much for reading! If you enjoyed this book, I'd love it if you'd consider leaving a review. Reviews give books greater visibility and a greater chance of getting found by more readers. This, in turn, gives authors a chance to write even more of the books you love.

About The Author

Andrea Knight

Andrea Knight's work is a celebration of the tangled dance between love and mystery, making her a standout author for anyone looking to lose themselves in stories where the flame of romance is kindled in the darkest of places. With each new release, she continues to push the boundaries of the genre, ensuring her place on the bookshelves of readers who love their tales of affection laced with a touch of danger.

Printed in Great Britain
by Amazon